"Can you explain what happened?" Akeem asked. "The intensity?"

Could she? Nine years had passed between them—a lifetime and still... No, she couldn't.

"My father had a lifetime of being reckless for his own amusement—"

"And you wanted a taste of it?"

"No," he denied, his voice a harsh rasp.

"Then what did you want?" Charlotte pushed.

"A night—"

"You risked your reputation for a night?" she cut him off. "And so far, it's been a disaster, and we haven't even got to bed." She blew out a puff of agitated air.

"Make no mistake," he warned, "things have changed."

"Changed?"

"My bed is off-limits."

She laughed, a throaty gurgle. "How dare you pull me from my life—fly me who knows how many miles into a kingdom I've never heard of and turn my words back on me!" She fixed him with an exasperated glare. "How dare you try to turn the tables on me!"

"If the tables have turned on anyone," he corrected, "it is me because you will be my wife."

Lela May Wight grew up with seven brothers and sisters. Yes, it was noisy, and she often found escape in romance books. She still does, but now she gets to write them, too! She hopes to offer readers the same escapism when the world is a little too loud. Lela May lives in the UK with her two sons and her very own hero, who never complains about her book addiction—he buys her more books! Check out what she's up to at lelamaywight.com.

This is Lela May Wight's debut book for Harlequin Presents—we hope that you enjoy it!

Lela May Wight

—

HIS DESERT BRIDE BY DEMAND

HARLEQUIN
PRESENTS

Recycling programs
for this product may
not exist in your area.

ISBN-13: 978-1-335-58369-7

His Desert Bride by Demand

Copyright © 2022 by Lela May Wight

For questions and comments about the quality of this book, please contact us at CustomerService@Harlequin.com.

Harlequin Enterprises ULC
22 Adelaide St. West, 41st Floor
Toronto, Ontario M5H 4E3, Canada
www.Harlequin.com

Printed in U.S.A.

HIS DESERT BRIDE BY DEMAND

Matthew, this one's for you.
Thank you for pushing me to dream, and dream big.
I love you.

A big thank you to my family. My baby girl, Lisa!
Thank you for being my cheerleader. Mom, thank
you for encouraging my love of words. Kim, Lou,
Luke, Ste and Josh, thank you for encouraging me
to run at my writing goals until I surpassed them.

Martin, Teresa, Amy and Joe, thank you for
believing in me.

My beautiful boys, thank you for believing in
Mommy and for giving me the time to write my
ABC's.

Frankie, thank you for your support and friendship
when the crows of doubt were ever present.

Shell, thank you for your friendship when I was a
newbie to the wonders of social media and the
romance book community.

Gwessie, thank you for sharing your joy of books
with me. Ride those unicorns hard, lovely lady.
The romance book community misses you dearly.

And last but not least, my editor, Charlotte. Thank
you for seeing the potential in my voice and for
making me a better writer.

PROLOGUE

THE BASTARD WAS DEAD.

Ripping free the report, Akeem crushed it and threw it across the room. And there, on a rug made from silk, lay a discarded account of Damien Hegarty's life and death, all summed up in a few paragraphs on expensive paper.

He almost chuckled. The man who'd called him a monster—*worse*—was dead, and this would be the closest Damien would ever get to opulence.

Relief should be the feeling easing the tension from Akeem's shoulders. But it wasn't.

*S*he would lose *everything*.

Akeem Abd al-Uzza, Crown Prince of Taliedaa, looked down again at the document he'd thought destroyed and his heart boomed in his ribcage.

There she was. A single photograph.

Charlotte.

He traced his finger along the outline of the woman in the picture. He remembered everything. Every minor detail of her softness against his rough. Oh, how he'd been obsessed by every blemish, every minor mark shadowing the golden tones of her flesh.

She had besotted him with her kindness.

'Kindness!' he sneered, and the word stung his lips.

Akeem raked unsteady fingers through his hair. Lust stormed through him, dredging up long-forgotten memories and stirring him in ways unexpected. *Undesired.*

The freckles above her right breast, and how he'd joined them together with his tongue before taking her nipple into his mouth. How she'd cried out his name—*his* name—as his hand explored her body for the first time the night before she'd rejected him. Thrown him away as if he was nothing.

He pushed back out of his chair to stalk to the window that revealed views of the ancient city below and the rolling deserts beyond.

It never lessened. The lurch in his gut as he looked down over the city. It would be his. It *was* his. He closed his eyes. He, the forgotten orphan heir, was the ruler, up on high in the palace in the mountains.

Why, for the love of all he had overcome, could he not leave the past alone?

Leave *her* alone?

Charlotte Hegarty had hurt him. She'd crushed all that was innocent within him. And yet, after almost a decade, he still wanted her.

Wildly.

Two weeks and he'd be officially named King. He had a limited amount of freedom left before the weight of the crown kept him firmly away from the past. *Away from her.* Away from his need to rub in her face all she'd thrown away to live a life of drudgery.

For one last time before he was King he would claim his revenge. It was the very personal act of a man, not a king, but it wasn't an opportunity he was going to miss.

Holding the past by the hand, he'd show it— and *her*—that there was no place in his world for either of them.

CHAPTER ONE

CHARLOTTE HEGARTY OPENED her palm and released the damp earth. Thud by thud it fell onto her father's coffin, deep brown against a beech veneer, and she felt...*nothing*. Numb. Completely empty.

Her flimsy ballet flats sank into the mossy ground as she turned her back on the grave and on the empty scene behind her. Empty all but for her and the vicar.

No one had bothered to show up. Not even his drinking buddies. *Friends* who were only ever there when the drinks were flowing... She took another step, and another, hating the feel of her too-thin blazer and the starched white shirt chafing against her skin. But she kept moving. Away from the past, from the hopes and dreams she'd laid at his feet. Time after time he'd squashed them, choosing the bottle over her. And in the end the bottle had won. It had taken him and any hope that one day he would turn around and *see* her.

His daughter.

The wake loomed in her mind, as big and dark as the large black ornate gates coming into view. She still hoped someone would remember him. Grieve for him. But there was no free bar at the wake. Only memories. Only pain. Only regrets. His friends didn't do real, did they? They didn't want to see the real-world consequences of their lifestyle.

She'd remember him for them.

Her last act as a dutiful daughter. She'd walk to the pub across the road, where she'd been given the back room for free, and pretend to eat the little triangle sandwiches filled with fish paste and cucumber. And then it would be over.

On heavy feet, she closed in on the wooden double doors in desperate need of paint, and opened them with unnecessary force.

She froze. Every atom of her being was suspended as her heart stopped pumping blood to her vital organs.

She'd conjured a ghost.

'Akeem?' His name left her gaping mouth before she'd processed…*him.* She took a step forward. 'You're here—it's you.'

'Here and in the flesh, Charlotte,' he confirmed, lazing back against the bar.

Her eyes locked on his mouth, to those full brown lips making each syllable of her name sound *wrong.* Just the way he'd made her feel nine years ago, when he'd reminded her of exactly who

she was. Charlotte Hegarty, unworthy of unconditional love. The daughter of an alcoholic, living in
the roughest end of London, surviving a poverty-
stricken life and barely functioning as a normal
sixteen-year-old should...

Bitterness swept through her and it made her
ache. Deep in her core.

Her name shouldn't be in his mouth or in his
mind.

He shouldn't be here.

But he was.

She unfurled herself, squaring her shoulders,
and locked her gaze on his. How appropriate, on
the day when there was nothing left to fight for
but herself, that he'd show up.

'Why are you here?'

She asked the question she'd spent countless
nights rehearsing this very scene with him. But
in her solo rehearsals she'd been the definition of
cool indifference as he'd begged her forgiveness.
The forgiveness she was going to pretend there
was no need for and send him on his way.

But she'd never expected it to actually happen—and definitely not today.

Akeem shrugged, one broad, black-sheathed
shoulder dipping to expose the pure breadth and
size of him. 'To offer my condolences.'

Indignant rage curled her toes. 'Still telling lies,
Akeem?' she accused, before the words had time
to linger in her mouth. He'd lied his way into her

bed and then left her behind without so much as a note.

His movements effortless, he pushed free from the age-stained bar. He was six feet plus of sheer male presence, closing in on her, and he was daring to smile. Full, gleaming white teeth in a sea of a short-cropped black beard.

'I never lied to you.'

The memory was vivid—visceral. It pulled her gaze back to his mouth, and to the last lie he'd spoken to her while climbing out of her bedroom window. He'd pressed a kiss to her swollen lips before sliding down to the porch roof with promises of tomorrow and for ever.

That lie had hurt the most.

'Whatever helps you sleep at night,' she countered, marvelling at the levelness of her tone.

'Sleep is for the dead.'

His long, lithe legs crossed the wooden floor and she couldn't breathe. His hair was thick and pushed to the side, as though he'd recently dragged his fingers through it.

He was breathtaking.

'I'm very much alive, and I never sleep.' He stopped, statue-still, in front of her.

Heat bloomed in her cheeks, down her throat, to spread out over her chest and deeper—*lower*. Her body recognised him before she could tell it not to. And she didn't like it. Not one bit. Because it was terrifying. This effect he had on her by simply being in the same airspace, stealing the air she needed to survive when he simply inhaled it.

'It must exhaust you, avoiding the demons haunting your bed.'

She planted her feet, readying herself to fight against a lifetime of remembering to keep quiet and do what had to be done. *Don't argue, don't fight—just to get on with it.* She'd been readying herself for this confrontation for nine long years. And she hated confrontation. But here it was.

Her moment.

His mouth flared into life. Not a grin, but a tilt of those sensuous lips as he leaned in. A hair's breadth away from her mouth, he whispered, 'My stamina has yet to be a concern.'

The air hissed from her lips. She knew what he was doing. He was intent on reminding her how she'd shared his bed. He had slept *then*. Wrapped around her like a second skin.

'What you do in your bed has nothing to do with me,' she said, Because it didn't—not any more. 'But you're not welcome here.'

'Am I not?'

His features were unmoved—a vision of innocence. But she knew better.

'No.' She moved her head from side to side in small, quick flicks. 'My father wouldn't have wanted you here, nor your condolences.'

'My condolences are for you,' he corrected, 'not him.'

'I'm surprised you have anything for *me*, let alone that you think of me,' she countered, and prepared herself for the bit she'd practised the most. The biggest and best lie. 'Because I don't think of you at all.'

If she'd felt nothing at the graveside she was feeling *everything* now. Her sixteen-year-old self was bursting out, reminding her twenty-five-year-old counterpart that it had unfinished business.

And here he was—*the unfinished business*—now undoing the top two pearl buttons at his neck. Slowly, he revealed his bronze throat, thick and pulsing inside the crisp white collar of his shirt.

He didn't respond. He simply watched her for a beat too long. His eyes searching hers. And a magnetic pull urged her to close the distance between them, to step inside the earthy scent of wood and sand and touch him.

The words had been easy, but what she hadn't expected was the primitive reaction her body was having to him. *This* wasn't part of the script. But she wouldn't show it! She wouldn't break on the outside, even if her insides were melting.

'I think of you often, *qalbi*,' he admitted, his voice low and soft, and she felt it like a physical caress on her cheek. 'I think of the life you chose.'

'The life I *chose*?' she repeated, and she hated the crack in her voice. It had been nine years. She couldn't blame him entirely that she'd stayed where he'd left her. But she did.

She pulled her lower lip between her teeth.

She blamed him for everything.

He nodded, his dark head dipping only once. 'This pitiful existence you call a life.'

'What?'

She stepped back then. Only slightly, but enough to give her room to strike him. Squarely, on that beautifully chiselled chin of his.

She knew how pitiful her life was, but— 'You have no right to judge my life,' she said, finishing her thought out loud.

'Don't I? You could have been anything. *Anything,*' he stressed. 'Instead you continued to nurse a man who belittled you at every chance he got for another decade.'

She blinked hard and fast. 'I…'

She could have been anything?

'I'm twenty-five,' she reminded him, 'not dead.'

But his words curdled in her gut, despite her feigned confidence. She didn't know what her life might have looked like now. She knew nothing apart from the all-consuming fact that she had no one and nothing to call her own.

'Tell me it's not true and regale me with your exciting plans now you are free. Are you still drawing?'

She gasped. *Drawing?* He remembered. He remembered the one part of herself that had allowed her freedom. Her pencil had been her ticket to adventure. *Her escape.* And she'd given it up.

Her drawing. Her art. Her one talent. Because her dad had called her drawings stupid, a waste of time when she should have been caring for him. He'd destroyed all her work. Crushed her dreams. And she'd let him because she'd felt selfish, taking those precious moments to draw and dream for herself.

How could she have taken time for herself when her dad had needed her help to survive? How could she have chased her foolish dream of becoming a portrait artist when her reality had been so heavy?

'Are you still chasing your dreams?' Akeem continued, and she swallowed the memory of what she'd lost. What her dad had taken from her. Not only her art, but her identity. Because the only thing that had defined who she was—not a daughter, not a carer—had been her art.

But quickly she had let her dreams go as if they'd never existed—what would have been the point of holding on to them?

She zeroed in on his face. On the man determined to make her remember. To make her regret.

His eyes, intense, were moving over her face. 'Or have you been wasting your life filling those empty whisky bottles with cold tea to fool your drunken father? Have you been wasting your life, *qalbi*, trying to save a man who did not want to be saved?'

He raised his hand, those long, elegant fingers

moving towards her cheek. She backed up, one step at a time. He was too close. *Too intimate.*

But his questions spoke to her at her deepest level of consciousness. Because she hadn't done—still wasn't doing—any of the things they'd whispered about late at night, hidden in her bedroom... those dreams and hopes of being...*more.*

Her insides twisted and snaked around her lungs.

Her dad had needed her when no one else had, even if he'd never recognised her sacrifice. Her time. Her art... He'd never seen that it was her keeping him alive and forgetting to live her own life. Never acknowledged how she'd managed their minimal income by getting to the bank before he did to withdraw their welfare benefit money before he spent it on whisky so they couldn't eat. He'd never seen her visiting food banks when she'd been too late and her father had taken the money before she had.

She'd made things work on a frayed string of hope and prayer, and not once had he thanked her. The daughter who had become the parent instead of the child. Who had worked in temporary jobs from catering, to retail, to office cleaning as soon as she had been old enough to get a job.

She'd worked in one meaningless job after another... She'd stood still for nine years. Exactly where Akeem had left her...

Her chest heaved.

She hadn't had a choice!

'I did what I had to,' she said, feeling the past snarling between them. 'I stood by my father as a daughter should.' She exhaled heavily, felt the cheap cotton of her shirt loosening on her chest. 'He was all I had left.'

'No,' he corrected, his voice laced with steel. 'Your father was all you *allowed* yourself to have.'

'Stop!' she demanded breathlessly.

She didn't want to hear this—any of it. This wasn't how it was supposed to go. *This wasn't it!* Why wasn't he on his knees, begging her forgiveness for leaving her behind?

'Are you the woman you wanted to be, Charlotte?' he asked, ignoring her.

She'd dared to believe she could be someone else once—that life had more to offer her than being her father's keeper—and Akeem had smashed those notions to smithereens. She had no clue who she was now, or what she was going to do. But she wouldn't admit that to him. It was hard enough to admit to herself that caring for her father had become her life.

'Stop,' she said again.

She rubbed forcibly at her exposed collarbone. She hated him. Hated what he'd done to her. Akeem had made her question everything. Not only question why he'd broken his promise to take her with him, but question herself on who she was and what she could never be. *And he still was!*

'Stop it, whatever this is, and leave.'

'But I've only just arrived.'

She glared at him. 'I didn't ask you to come.'

'You'd rather mourn alone—' he spread his hands wide, arching a thick dark brow '—in a room like this?'

'How graceful of you to remind me.' She smiled unkindly. 'But you have no right to tell me how to grieve.'

'All you should feel is relief.' His nostrils flared, but she watched him shutter the exasperation glazing his eyes. 'But you're right,' he conceded. 'I have no right to tell you how to grieve, or where, because I am not sorry he is dead. But I am sorry you have lost your father, Charlotte,' he continued, keeping his voice low and firm. 'I know you loved him for reasons I'll—'

'This is not the time.'

'What better time is there?' he asked.

She watched the white shirt and black jacket becoming taut over his shoulders, hinting at the hard and muscular body beneath. The body she'd once coveted so wantonly.

Letting out a harsh breath, she uncurled her hands and scrubbed them across her face. It was time to end this.

'What do you want?'

He closed in, removing the space she'd created between them. 'It's not what I want that matters. It's what I have that you need, Lottie.'

'What is it that I *need*, Akeem?' she echoed back at him. His use of the name he'd used to call her by was doing things to her insides she didn't want to recognise.

'You need me.'

'*You?*' she whispered, disgusted that her body was having such a visceral reaction to his statement.

'Yes.' He smiled, his brown eyes burning black. '*Me*. Akeem Abd al-Uzza.' His voice, deep and proud, oozed masculinity. *Power*.

'Not Akeem Ali?' she asked.

'Abd al-Uzza is my father's name.'

'Your dad's? But your mum—'

She closed her eyes. It didn't matter. She didn't want to know. He'd given up his name just as he'd given her up. Abandoned them both as if they meant nothing.

Forcing herself to chuckle, she tilted her head. 'Akeem Ali—' she shrugged '—or Abd al-Uzza, I don't want you here, and I certainly don't need you.'

'Today is the beginning of the rest of your life. What better way to start that new life than with a night of pleasure in my arms, surrounded by opulence?'

'You want to take me to bed?' she spluttered.

'Yes. You will spend one night in my bed—one night of extreme pleasure.'

'*Why?*'

'Call it what you will—*closure*…' he stretched the word.

'Closure?' Her heart hammered. 'You came here uninvited because you thought I'd sleep with you one last time for *closure*?' Her eyes widened, and she hooked a brow. 'How very arrogant of you.'

'Does my arrogance surprise you when I can see your pulse pounding wildly beside the hollow of your throat?'

'Yes.' She nodded. 'The boy I knew would ask—never demand.'

Unbidden, memory claimed her. The swipe of tentative fingers across her naked hipbone. The press of his mouth behind her ear as he asked if she liked his hand there…did she want him to bring her pleasure with his fingers?

She shuddered. Her Akeem had been gentle, caring—never demanding. The Akeem she had known was not this man standing in front of her.

'I am not the boy you remember.' His voice was silk. Seductive. 'The pleasure you will experience in my arms will be unlike any you've known before or after me.'

He raised his hand and applied pressure to the frantic beating at her throat. It took everything she had in her arsenal not to react to his touch and to remain indifferent. But she wasn't indifferent. She'd only ever known *him*. All she could do was watch—feel all the things she shouldn't be feeling.

She hated him, didn't she?

'Should I put my mouth here, so you may understand the power of attraction still between us?'

'No!' she shrieked, unable to breathe or to think about anything but her disloyal body. It tingled from the intensity of his gaze—his touch. And she wanted to step into his embrace.

What was wrong with her? It was the day of her father's funeral. She was on the edge. And here was Akeem, magnifying her overwrought emotions to fever-pitch. She couldn't stand it. His ability to still affect her. He would not trick her into forgetting what he'd done. How he'd abandoned her.

'No,' she said again, 'my bed is off-limits to you.'

'It's not *your* bed I want you in,' he corrected. 'It's mine.'

'Whatever bed,' she huffed, knowing he'd purposely missed her point. 'I won't be in it with you,' she declared, and hoped she meant it. 'You're the one that needs this.' She waved her hands. 'Not me. Otherwise you wouldn't be here.'

'You need to close the door on the past as much as I do,' Akeem concluded, and moved his thumb up the taut lines of her throat. With his forefinger beneath her chin, he tilted her head. 'Take a chance and come to bed with me.'

Temptation teased through her, and the knot in her abdomen was an acknowledgment of the desire she felt. She didn't need his mouth on her skin to understand that whatever was still between them was powerful—more than it had been nine years ago. But it was different—stronger. An older kind of yearning… It was lust, she recognised. *Desire*.

She was a fool.

'No,' she whispered, and his hands fell away to his side. 'I can't.'

'Fear stopped you when you were a girl, and now you are a woman—' his eyes swept over her '—you're still scared.'

'How so?' she asked, because he'd been the one to run away. He'd been the one who was afraid.

'What do you have to lose?' he asked, and she bit back the immediate response clinging to the inside of her mouth.

Nothing.

'You have no job, no family, no money, and soon you'll be homeless. Do you wish to remain exactly where you have always been until they forcibly evict you from everything you know? Your house? Your home?'

'How do you know that?'

'It is easy to imagine the life you have led.' His lips thinned, and silently he held her gaze.

Of course he knew everything. He was a man of means now. She recognised it in every stitch of his handmade suit. He knew she hadn't moved forward. To him, she was still the same girl he'd known. Scared, and alone, and thrust into a system she had been frightened would take her away from her dad.

She'd always kept her mouth shut. As her dad had taught her. Outsiders didn't matter. Outsiders didn't count. And she had told no one anything—not even the police who'd hammered on the door because the school hadn't been able to contact her dad for three days and they'd had concerns for her welfare. They'd found her dad barely conscious. The social services team had delivered her to a children's home, and still she'd remained silent. But she had told Akeem.

Eight weeks, they'd told her. An interim care order. If in eight weeks her dad could prove he was well enough to take care of her, she could go home. For those eight weeks it had been her and him. Akeem and Charlotte.

He'd been her first and only friend. She'd opened up for the first time in her life—because he'd offered her something she'd never had. Friendship.

But she wasn't that girl any more. She didn't want to be. Because *that* girl had given everything to her father until there had been nothing left for her.

A recklessness she'd never known before pulsated through her. Urging her to throw caution to the wind and admit that his touch on her body was welcome and she wanted more. *Much more*. Because when had she ever been selfish? Or allowed herself to behave any way rather than steadfastly, working out the pros and cons first?

Once was the simple answer. Once when she'd packed her suitcase, ready to run away with Akeem, and he'd gone without her...

She had nothing to lose by spending the night with him.

Only pleasure—however fleeting.

Every muscle in her body strained as she moved towards him and stood on tiptoe.

'One night?' she hissed and waited, nose to nose, eye to eye, for him to respond—like a boxer squaring off against an opponent before a fight, just as her dad had done in his youth.

The only time her father had fought for anything it had been for those few trophies on the mantelpiece at home. He'd never fought for her. For their family. The only things he'd taken pride in had been his boxing achievements. And what did *she* have to be proud of? A few awards for her portraits from secondary school? An unconditional place to study for a diploma at college she'd never taken up because she'd had to get a job instead? She'd had to take care of her dad...

'Yes.' Akeem agreed, his eyes hungry, his breathing shallow. 'One night.'

It was desire. That was all. Right now, she needed to connect, and she was reacting to the havoc of the day and to the storm of emotions he was evoking inside her. The indulgence of being impulsive was equally as exciting as it was frightening, but she was surrendering to it. To a spontaneity she'd never been allowed to have.

Until now.

Her hands had made their way to the solid wall of his chest. The fabric of his shirt was cushioning her fingers. She pushed away and stepped out of his embrace.

'Let's get it over with,' she said, trying on for size the indifference she wanted to project. But she wasn't indifferent. She was excited. Scared. Slick in places she shouldn't be.

His eyes narrowed. 'As you wish. But we will not "get it over with". It will be long and gratifying.'

Tingles shot through her. 'One night and one night only. Then we part ways. Nothing changes. We'll be the same as we are now. A distant memory in each other's life.'

'Yes,' he agreed, his beautiful face carved in granite.

Charlotte hesitated. He was lying. *Again.* Or was she? Because it would change everything. It would change *her.* But wasn't that what she wanted? To be completely brand-new and forging forward into a shiny future, not beholden to the past?

'No more thinking, Charlotte,' he said, his voice gruff, and he extended his arm. 'Take my hand.'

With bated breath, she did.

Blindly, she followed him. Took his hand, without pause and without question. To be deposited neatly into a waiting car.

She looked at him, folded against the leather interior, seemingly oblivious to her presence, and her traitorous heart did a double beat. Her hand still burned. Her palm still radiated the heat of their hands' union. And her mouth…oh, her mouth…it throbbed with the memory of his lips so close to hers.

Her heart threatening to explode, she looked away from him. Sweat beaded her palms and she smoothed them down her black pencil skirt. There was a ladder in her tights. A run where thigh met knee. She pulled at it. She didn't belong here, with her cheap skirt and ninety-nine pence tights.

This wasn't how a woman should look on her way to a hotel to be seduced.

She turned to the window. The scene beyond was a whizzing blur.

Her clothes didn't matter. She wanted this. She wanted *him*.

Keeping her back to him, she felt the warmth of his breath hit her nape before he moved his mouth to her ear.

'So tense…'

A soft but firm finger traced the outline of her spine, and she shivered as a heavy sensation dragged through her in its wake.

'I have every intention of easing this tension.'

She hadn't been touched in almost a decade. She didn't need to ask what he meant. Of course there'd been dates. She'd worked in endless jobs, and meeting people hadn't been the problem. But she'd never connected with them, never wanted them, because their lips hadn't been *his* lips.

They hadn't given her *this*. Whatever this was still burning hotly between them.

Arching her neck, she leaned into him and closed her eyes. One night—that was all—and his hands would be everywhere... On her—in her. They'd be naked and anonymous in some swanky London hotel. She *needed* this. He was right. She needed *him*.

The car slowed to an almost-crawl. Or was she slowing down? She didn't seem to be breathing—just *feeling*.

'Does it scare you?' she asked.

He pressed his chest against her back. Strength surged from him. Solid and all-consuming confidence.

'Does what scare me?'

She twirled in his embrace, splaying her hand against his seemingly impenetrable chest, keeping him at bay, although every instinct told her to pull him in. Grab him by the lapels and pull him in. Closer.

'This energy between us?'

'What I feel is excitement,' he admitted, 'not fear.'

'Me too,' she whispered truthfully. 'But it's been nearly ten years.' She grappled with her tongue. 'We are strangers, and yet…'

'We are *strangers*?'

'How can we not be? I was only sixteen when we met at St John's Children's—'

'I was nearly eighteen.' His eyes widened. 'We were both innocents, finding solace in each other.'

'But the trajectory of our lives since then has been…' She wanted to say *different*, but it didn't feel right.

He vibrated luxury. The suit caressing his body. The car. He'd moved on to bigger and better things and she—

She shook her head and looked at her hand touching his chest. Crashing into this flesh and muscle nine years ago at the children's home had opened a whole new world for her. They'd become each other's secret. They'd been each other's escape.

Akeem had offered her companionable silence in a world that had refused to be quiet, offered her comfort in the endless task of worrying about her dad by just letting her be still with him. They'd sat watching TV in the communal lounge, or talking in the garden, and she'd offered him a reprieve too, from the care system he'd been so eager to escape, by listening to his dreams. He'd wanted to build. That had been his dream. To go from labouring on a renovation site to building skyscrapers in the sky.

She'd never imagined that nearly a decade later this was where she'd be. A stranger to him.

Her fingers moved of the own volition. Testing the firmness—the *realness*—of him.

She'd wanted a family to call her own…a career that fulfilled her fanciful dream of becoming a portrait artist… And then the one person who'd believed in her dreams had vanished and so had they. Her dreams. Vanished as soon as she'd dared to believe they were possible.

Charlotte encircled the pearl button in the middle of his shirt with the pad of her thumb. Lifting her gaze, she eyed him cautiously, the pink tip of her tongue poking through her mouth to moisten her lower lip.

Akeem had made her *believe*.

She swallowed—hard. He'd made her believe in lots of falsities. Her breath caught and she pushed a finger inside the buttonhole. Her finger met a fine fuzz of hair. And heat.

But this was real.

This want.

'You know me,' he declared. 'You still want me and you are looking for a way to justify your desire. The connection still between us should dispel any shame attached to spending the night with me.'

She gasped, unable to contradict his pinpoint

accuracy over her tumultuous emotions. Could he read her so easily? Could he *see* her?

'We are *not* strangers,' he continued. 'Your body knows mine.' He placed the pad of his thumb on her top lip and instinctively she opened her mouth to accept him. He pulled his hand away and reached for hers, placed it on the hard length of him beneath his trousers. 'And my body knows yours.'

She couldn't move. The heat of him mesmerised her. The hardness. The open conviction with which he wanted her.

'There is no shame or guilt to be found here, *qalbi*,' he promised, 'only pleasure.'

She didn't answer. Couldn't. And the silence stretched, palpable with the heaviness between them.

'We've arrived,' he informed her, nodding towards the window.

And before she'd caught her breath he was opening the door on her side and offering her his hand. She stepped out to join him.

Planes.

They were everywhere she looked. Small ones, big ones, and some bigger still.

She rounded on him. 'Where's the hotel?'

'There was never a hotel.'

'Then where—?' A plane in the distance took flight, and she watched as it ascended into the skies. How had they got to an airport?

Her heart hammering, she turned her eyes on him. 'You said one night?'

'Yes,' he confirmed. 'For one night I mean to have you in my bed. There is no trickery at play. No deception.' His voice was low. Gruff. '*My bed.* Not one anyone else has enjoyed, and one where only my body knows the dips and springs.'

'Sounds like you need a new mattress!'

A sting of heat worked its way from her chest to slash across her cheeks. She was reacting to him. Her traitorous body had hardened and softened in places she'd forgotten could melt with the mere sound of his voice.

'I need *you*, *qalbi*,' he contradicted. 'And I mean to have you in my bed. In my desert kingdom.'

'What?' Her heart hiccupped. '*Your* desert kingdom?'

'I am Crown Prince Akeem Abd al-Uzza, son of the late King Saleem Abd al-Uzza and soon to be named King of Taliedaa.'

'*How?*' Her mouth gaped as she reeled from his announcement. 'When your birth father contacted you on your eighteenth birthday I thought—'

'You thought wrong. It was not my parent who contacted me. It was my father's senior aide, who'd been watching over me my entire life. Waiting.'

'Waiting for what?' Anger replaced her shock. 'To see how much life could kick you?'

She knew how much life had kicked them both.

And he was saying someone could have saved him from that. But hadn't.

'Your first thought is how it was unfair to *me*?' Thick brows arched over coolly observant eyes. 'And not what *you* could have become?'

'What *I* could have become? It's not about me…' she dismissed easily, with a wave of her wrist. 'He left you—*a child*—alone to fend for yourself when you are of *royal blood*? You're a *prince*—' she pressed a trembling hand to her chest '—and they let you be tossed from children's home to foster home to children's home again because they were…*waiting*?'

'Spare me your pity, Charlotte. I do not need or want it.'

'It's not pity I'm feeling.' And it wasn't. It was hot rage, with a cooling dose of empathy.

Red lines shadowed his high cheekbones. 'Then do not look at me with those eyes.'

'They're the only eyes I've got.' She shook her head. 'Why did they—*he*,' she corrected, 'wait so long after your mother died?'

'My mother was of no consequence to the crown.'

'Wasn't she a secret royal, too?'

'No.' The response was dry—husked. 'My mother was a plaything of my father's—a commoner working in the palace. She left my father's kingdom the minute she discovered she was pregnant for fear of being ostracised.' Harshness contorted his face. '*Her* death changed nothing.'

The confession was low and deep. She could see how much it had cost him to admit that.

Confusion narrowed her eyes. 'What about you? Why did they leave you in the care system until your eighteenth birthday?'

'Kings do not trouble themselves with their bastard sons unless they are a security risk or they suddenly need them.'

He hadn't said *want* and that chafed at her skin.

Had they both been unwanted by their fathers?

'Which were you?'

'I was—I *am*,' he emphasised, 'the only heir by blood to the Taliedaaen throne.'

His voice was toneless. Not proud. Not…*anything.* Her eyes flicked across his features. Vacant.

A heaviness expanded in her core. 'Why didn't you tell me?'

'Would it have made a difference?' he asked. 'I told you the truth. My birth family got in contact and wanted to meet me. Would the rest of it have mattered?' His eyes, black and granite, held hers.

'Of course not.' The denial was hot in her mouth. 'But we were planning to elope—'

'You promised yourself to a boy with callused hands. A boy who worked from dawn till dusk in manual labour to learn his trade.' His face was unreadable, a mask of emptiness. 'You did not promise yourself to an orphan prince raised in poverty, who would one day be a king. You wanted the man and not the crown. There was no need to tell you.'

'Is that why it was such a rush? Your plan to meet my dad? To tell him we were leaving, with or without his consent? Because you weren't only leaving London, you were leaving England altogether? Is that why you left—' She cut herself off and trapped the last words in her mouth.

Without me?

'When I suggested we run away together—run away from a system that had cared for neither of us and away from your father—I was taking us to a bedsit with the leaving care grant they'd offer me on my eighteenth birthday. But that day I was going home. To my country. It was that day or never. Because I was leaving and I wasn't coming back.'

We? Us?

'And you chose never?' she asked quietly, his choice of words making her gut churn.

'*I* didn't choose. But I'm here now.'

She wanted to push. Wanted him to say to her face that she hadn't been enough. That she hadn't been princess material and he'd forged on without her. But the words clung to her throat.

That was *why* he'd left her behind. He'd abandoned her because he'd believed she wasn't capable or worthy of his new life. He'd known the daughter of an alcoholic would never be accepted by royalty. *By his family.* Or anyone, really.

She was unlovable—destined to fail. Just as her dad had reminded her every time she'd got something wrong. No, more often than that—every time she'd breathed too loudly, spoken too confidently.

Her chest ached for the girl she'd been. The girl who'd poured all her simple hopes and dreams into his ear. Believing he was accepting her as she was. For *who* she was.

'I can't go to Taliedaa,' she said, ignoring the past nagging at her in the bitter depths of her memories. She wanted to close the door on the past—not wrench it open! 'I don't want to go to a world where you're a crown prince and I'm... *me.*' She looked down at the splintering fabric on her knee. 'I have ladders in my tights. I can't possibly get on a plane.'

His gaze locked on hers. 'Then take them off.'

She gasped. 'I...' Exhaling heavily, she shrugged. 'I can't.'

And she couldn't. Because she might take off her tights, but she couldn't take off her skin. She couldn't shrug off who she was. And she couldn't change who he was now.

'Where will you go, *qalbi*?' he asked. 'Back to the same little house where we became lovers?'

'Once hardly makes us lovers,' she responded stiffly.

'I stand corrected,' he said placatingly, and there were those teeth again. Perfect in their insincere symmetry. 'The same little house where we spent countless hours hiding from your father—hiding from that robotic children's home manager—to *talk*.'

He didn't blink, those eyes holding fast to hers, and her stomach flipped. Painfully.

His smile faded. 'The same little house where I lost my virginity and you lost yours.'

Her breath caught tightly in her lungs. Memories claimed her. Just as he'd intended. Memories of the one and only time they'd made love. Of the night they'd surrendered their virginities to one another to seal their pact to marry. It had been the night before they'd agreed to tell her dad. The night before they would leave together and never return.

Instead he'd left her behind, with her father full of *'I told you so,'* because she'd strayed from the plan and told her dad everything before Akeem would arrive.

And he never had.

'I am not that boy any more,' he reminded her again, and reached for her. His fingers held lightly to the tops of her arms. 'I will not fumble or hesitate.' His eyes darkened. 'My touch will be... *controlled*.'

'You were never out of control.' Charlotte stared at him. 'Not with me.'

He released her. 'Wasn't I...?' He continued without a reflective pause. 'It matters not, because the pleasure you will experience in my arms now will be nothing like our night together. It will be...' He exhaled sharply, his nostrils flaring. 'It will be full of the pleasure only a king can give you. Only me. Only what I have become.'

'King?' she croaked.

'This is your last chance,' he warned, ignoring her question. 'Get in—' he stood aside, waving his hand towards the long red carpet leading up to a gigantic plane's entrance '—or stay exactly where you have always been.'

He dropped his hand to his side, turned and walked towards the plane.

'Wait!'

He snapped his head back round. 'Wait?'

Her heart slammed against her ribs, the breath in her lungs choking her. The funeral had been for her dad. The wake had become all about Akeem. But *this...*

This could be for her.

'I'm not the girl you remember, either.'

And she wasn't. She didn't want to be. She wasn't a secret royal, but she wanted to be someone else, if only for a minute. She wanted to be selfish. Bold.

Worthy of...*more.*

Her gut was gripped in a tight fist. She would never be her father. She wouldn't allow herself to let life pass her by again. Her father had been nothing more than a shadow on the doorstep of death for far too long, and he'd been dead long before she'd found him.

A heart attack brought on by alcoholism and no one had been there. *She* hadn't been there. He'd died because she'd failed to do the one thing she'd been trying to do her whole life. Keep him alive.

Closing the memory down before it consumed her, Charlotte focused hard on the man before her. The living flesh of a man offering her *life*.

She was alive. She could live. The only person she had left to fail now was herself. And she was tired of failing.

Shaking her waist-length curls behind her back, she moved ahead of him, keeping her head high.

She was getting on board.

CHAPTER TWO

AKEEM HAD LIED.

The royal plane was a hotel. The double-decker private jet was the largest and fastest ever to take to the skies. He could have her right here, right now, in a multitude of rooms. Send her back to her insignificant life with only the marks he'd leave on her body with no one being the wiser. He'd bite and suck, and—

Beast.

His hand gripped the metal rail. Breaking his rhythm behind her.

The word was a murmur in his mind. An echo of the name his father had called his only son— his only child—and yet it scraped across his skin.

He was not feral any more. He did not cry when he was sad. He did not shout when he was angry. He was not the boy who, gifted with a small stuffed toy, had taken it to his room and torn the legs off. He was not the teenager who had answered with his fists when the boys in his class had mocked his trousers with their worn-out knees and his yellowing shirts.

He was not the boy who had been presented to his father, which had unleashed in him a rage knitted so tightly into his being that he'd scared himself. Even with guards holding his wrists above his head, his anger had swelled inside him. Bigger than him. Stronger. Untamed and ferocious.

No, he was not that boy any more, and he did not give in to his basic needs on a whim.

This was strategic, he reminded himself, shutting out the memory of those guards and his father's voice. He moved faster, urging her up the stairs. This one night was planned. *Necessary.* Seduce and destroy. Not only Charlotte, but the past, and any lingering remains of the boy he could never be again. The boy nobody had wanted. The boy his father had forbidden him to be.

Watching the gentle sway of her hips, he followed behind her as she climbed the stairs and entered the palatial aeroplane. There were no staff to greet them. Under his orders. No one would see her. No one would know. *Only him.*

She was his last tie to the past and he would sever that rope.

He stayed in sync with her every move as she tentatively padded onto the brilliant white carpet stretching the length of the first small lounge and acting as her personal runaway. Tight curls kissed the hollow at the base of her spine that he'd known so well. She was undoubtedly curvier. Even from behind, in that awful black blazer, he could see the swell of her hips and the prominent dip of her waist.

'Akeem?'

Her voice was gentle. Hesitant. She didn't turn. Simply stopped. Looking ahead and not behind. He'd spent nearly a decade trying not to look back. Not to feel. *Think.* But she'd always been there. Taunting him.

'Keep going,' he insisted, and after a brief hesitation she walked through the next open door in its gilded frame and entered the main salon.

With a press of a button the obscured glass came together as double doors behind them. His heartbeat raged to a deafening crescendo, so fast it almost hurt.

She was all his now.

Charlotte halted, and moved her head from side to side, taking in the shuttered windows lining the walls, the plush sofas draped in beige and gold running along each wall. A sound of awe escaped her, and he felt himself swell.

Open-mouthed, she drank in the surroundings he lived in every day. The slashes of light carefully designed to illuminate the highly polished wooden panels and hand-carved tables. Everything shimmered with a gold hue—including her.

She was looking straight ahead, and he watched her gaze stall. *The throne.* High-backed, and made from the finest yellow metal, encrusted with Taliedaa's very own rare jewels.

She gasped, and the sound was thrilling. He only wished his mouth was on hers so he could taste it. Taste the sweet taste of victory from her plush little mouth.

'Sit, *qalbi*,' he ordered.

Big green eyes turned to him. 'But *where*?'

Where did she think?

He strode towards her, backing her up into the only place she *could* sit. The throne with its clawed feet. It hadn't been designed for comfort. It had been created to bring everyone's attention in the room to the person who sat on it.

It was *his* throne now. And he wanted his eyes on nothing but her. Because only for today—only for one night—she would taste and feel everything that belonged to him. Recognise everything he had become. That he *would* become.

A king.

Her hands pinched together in front of her. *'Here...?'*

Akeem leant towards her and reached down beside her waist to grasp the seatbelt.

'I can do it,' she said, and her fingers brushed against his as she tried to take it from him. She stilled, craning her neck to look into his eyes.

He'd felt it too.

The surge.

'Allow me,' he said, pulling it around her and clipping it closed.

Licking her plump lips, she drew his gaze. He followed her tongue as it moistened the outline of those lips he'd dreamt of too often in the night's dark.

His eyes moved over her face. From the slight crevice below her nose to her high cheekbones. To her eyes. A deep emerald-green with slashes of gold highlighting her right iris. He had not forgotten those eyes. But he would.

Soon there would be no more dreams.

'Outside…' she started. 'You said King? Not Prince?'

He stiffened. 'My father passed away a few weeks ago and I will take his role as King, officially, in two weeks.' With one last tug, he fastened her tightly into the seat.

'I'm sorry for your loss,' she said.

But he wasn't sorry.

'As I am for yours,' he said instead.

'We're both alone now.'

She offered him a small smile, and it was a punch straight to his solar plexus. *Kindness.* He didn't want it. He didn't need it. Not any more. But he didn't move. Didn't speak. For fear she would somehow see the boy he'd spent nine years outgrowing. Pushing him into the shadows. Closing the lid…

'What was he like?' she asked.

His mouth gaped. 'Who?'

'Your dad.'

His jaw tensed. 'He was a king.'

'I know that.' She frowned. 'But was your dad everything you thought he would be?'

'No,' he answered honestly. 'He was a selfish man and a selfish king.'

'That's so sad—'

'No. It is anything but sad, Charlotte,' he corrected, keeping his voice low. Neutral. 'He taught me what not to be.'

Him, he added silently.

'How did he teach you?' she asked. 'Were there lessons in royal protocol?'

He nodded, pressing his teeth together.

'Were they hard?'

'I received my first lesson on arrival in Taliedaa. It was the toughest and the most successful,' he said, avoiding the impulse to grip his wrists, where he could still feel the pressure of his father's guards holding him.

He blamed her, he realised. Blamed her for the anger he'd travelled with to meet his father.

You let yourself get attached to her.

He *had* let himself, he corrected.

He was attached to nothing and no one now.

But the day he'd arrived in Taliedaa he'd been hurting from her rejection.

He'd asked his father why he hadn't rescued him from poverty the moment they'd presented him to the King. But it wasn't only that he'd been asking about. He hadn't been so naïve even as the boy he was. He hadn't only been asking why his father had forgotten him. He'd wanted to know why they'd all abandoned him. His mother... The foster families...

Charlotte.

His father had answered him. Told him in no uncertain terms why he'd never come for him before. Why they'd all abandoned him. Because nobody wanted pathetic little boys or pitiful young men. He had been born into weakness, he had told him, and it was his nature to surrender to it. To be weak.

Like his mother.

Akeem had flown at him. In a heartbeat he'd unleashed a lifetime of hurt on the man—his father. Wounded. Crying. Screaming. The royal guards had caught him by the wrists and raised his arms above his head and the King had laughed.

There he had been, face to face with his father as he sat on his pretty throne, surrounded by men who would protect him with their lives, and every time Akeem had struggled, or sworn, he had instructed them to hit him—*harder.*

He had fought. He had cursed. And they had hit him with closed fists.

His father had had the clothes striped from his body to show him how primitive he was. He'd told him that he responded to his urges without thought or reason, acting on impulse like a basic dog, rather than thinking through his situation or how to respond to it to gain the best outcome for himself.

He was worse than a dog, the King had said, because dogs responded to stimulus. Akeem was a beast. Primitive. Untamed and useless.

His father had given him a choice. Forget the boy he was and the man he was becoming or go home. Back to his little English life. To his *basic* life.

Akeem's outburst had meant nothing. His father had used it as a teaching tool. The only reason his father had sought him out, wanted to place him on the throne, was for his own ego. To continue his bloodline, however diluted or illegitimate, because he'd sired no other children.

'What was it? The lesson?' Charlotte asked, dragging him back to the reason she was here.

To see the person he was now. Rich. Powerful. Different not only in name, but in body, in mind. He'd chosen to become Akeem Abd al-Uzza, Crown Prince of Taliedaa. There had been no other choice.

Be nothing—unwanted—or become someone else.

A prince.

He didn't shout any more.

'It was a lesson to leave Akeem Ali behind.'

Charlotte nodded. 'He wanted his son to have

his name. Understandable…' She narrowed her eyes. 'But didn't you want to keep it?'

'That was not an option.'

'But surely your dad must have understood how important your mother was to you? If not to him?'

'All my father cared for was himself.'

'And his people? Surely he cared for them?' she asked, pushing for answers he didn't want to give.

He didn't want to tell her the disgusting parts of the King's life. The open sex. Women draped all over him in full view of his men. The greed. Wanting his toys faster—shinier—while his people suffered. The total disregard for his people's needs. His country.

His son.

'He cared for nothing but himself,' he repeated.

'What about you? Do *you* care?'

'I will not be the man or the King my father was,' he answered, each word measured and truthful, despite his need to rub his position in her pretty little face. 'I will claim his title and make it mine. I will not be *a* king,' he summarised for her. 'I will be *the* King, and my people will come first as they never did under my father's rule.'

And he would do it as he had been doing things for nine years. Small steps. Small choices. Small changes. His people first. His needs… *Never.*

Until today? a voice mocked.

He pushed it aside. One day was all he wanted. Twenty-four hours to claim his revenge as a man, to take what he needed and close the door on the past for ever. Only then could he be the King his people needed.

'We are the mirror image of each other,' she said.

His brows pulled together. 'How?'

'You lost a mother you loved,' she continued, 'and I lost a father.'

'Do you compare what I felt for my mother with what *you* felt for your father?'

'Yes,' she answered simply. 'You loved your mother unconditionally. I know you were young when she died, but you spoke about her with pure idolisation. I know if you could've stopped her getting into that carcass of a car you would have. You would have kept her safe. I never idolised my dad, but I loved him. I tried to keep him safe, too.'

His eyes widened. 'And my father?'

'Absent—like my mum. She left me with my dad, as your father left you with your mother.'

'We are not the same.'

'I said mirror images—reverse. *Opposites.*'

She was right. They belonged to different worlds. But they had started out from a similar place. A point of reference they could both identify with.

He'd even dared to *love* her once.

His face contorted, his mouth twisting into a snarl, and he turned away from her. He knew better now—much better.

Love was an absurd ideology for the weak. It was a basic emotion and he would never let himself be primitive again. He wanted her. He acknowledged that. But it was physical closure he needed. No feelings. No emotion. Just sex and her recognition that he was no longer the boy she'd rejected.

Akeem sat on the sofa facing her, clipped himself in, and watched. He observed her as the man he'd taught himself to be. As a king would—with open appreciation.

'Are you just going to sit there and gawk at me?' she asked.

'Yes.'

Golden flecks burned in a sea of green as, back straight, knees together, she looked straight ahead and over his head, as if nothing could faze her. He smiled. He'd ruffle more than her inhibitions. He'd crush them to dust.

His legs spread, he lounged back. Here she was, within reach—not a photograph put on his desk with a breakdown of her yearly routines. She was tangible, with an energy he could taste.

'Charlotte?' he said, when she closed her eyes as the plane reached a furious speed.

She didn't respond as the plane climbed higher, nose-first, but held tighter to her knees and drew his attention to her ripped tights and exposed skin.

His world now was far removed from hers, with inexpensive stockings and shoes, with barely any soles on the shoes cradling her small feet. But he'd known that world with mended clothes, and he hated the reminder of who he'd been with her.

His jaw clenched, because it wasn't her clothes that were making him uncomfortable but the memories hurtling towards him, too fast to catch them. Because with her he'd been everything his father had told him he wasn't.

He'd been... *Calm.* She'd soothed him. Stroked the unnourished ego of a boy who hadn't known such arresting tranquillity before. Not since his mother. Not with the temporary families they'd placed him with, who'd all sent him back with a note to say he was too quiet, too tearful, too loud, too angry—*too broken.* The behavioural mentors who'd tried to draw him out of himself—out of his head—had given up when he'd made little progress and had still spoken louder with his fists than with his words.

The palace guards had held his wrists as his father had called out with every punch that the boy he was, was unwanted. With her, it hadn't taken vile words or clenched fists to stop his rage. It had only taken *her.* Her presence to soothe the anger in his gut. The anger he'd taught himself to hide, to replace with the determination to succeed.

But he wasn't calm now.

The temptation to rip the fabric from her legs rocketed through him, heating his blood.

But he would never be part of *that* world again.

A tightness he hadn't realised was clinging to his muscles was released.

They were airborne.

He clenched his jaw. The shoes. The tights. The clothes. She'd stayed in the world of *make do*, and yet she sat on his throne as regally as a queen.

He shifted, clamping his lips into a thin slit. Did he know *this* Charlotte? It didn't matter. For twenty-four hours she would forget her world of minding the pennies. And he would enjoy exposing her to every delight of the flesh and then send her back with only regret on her lips.

He sat forward, taking in her paleness, the concealed tension revealing itself in every line of her delectable body. He stood, closing the space between them, and unclipped her seatbelt.

She opened her eyes. Heat and want bloomed inside him instantly. He pushed a long lock of curls behind her ear. 'Are you airsick?'

A flush appeared on her high cheekbones. 'I've never flown before.'

She wasn't unwell—she was overwhelmed.

Thrusting an expletive from his mind, he pulled her into step beside him, and for his every large step Charlotte took two.

'Where are you taking me?'

He noted her breathlessness, the tightness laced through her fingers, as they moved through the next set of doors to a long corridor that splintered off into the master bedrooms.

'To show you to your room.'

'Don't you have staff to do that?'

He stopped and turned to her. 'You are only to be seen by me.'

He pushed open a door, and with a tug of his wrist pulled her into the room ahead of him. He lingered in the doorway as she took in her surroundings. Her gaze paused on the large bed. His eyes went to it too, and everything in him urged him to move into the room and push her down into the mattress, with his weight firmly between her thighs.

She turned to face him, her back towards the bed. 'Why can no one see me?' she asked, snapping him out of the heat pooling in his loins.

'You'll enter my kingdom in secret and leave before it's discovered that you arrived.'

'I'm to be sneaked in and out?'

'Of course,' he agreed.

Not a flicker of indecency haunted the velvet richness of his voice, but he felt it. The sticky fingers of doubt where triumph should be. Because to act so selfishly was close to being everything he did not want to be.

Like his father.

You are your father's son.

'Why the cloak and dagger?' Her brows knitted together. 'Surely even a king has needs?'

'My father blatantly took women to his bed, flaunted his affairs and mocked his people with his hedonistic pursuits, because he put his needs before his country—' He cut himself off. He'd told her too much.

'And you don't want to be a king who does that?'

'No,' he agreed, and let his lungs fully deflate before dragging in a deep, silent breath through his nostrils. This was nothing like his father's pleasurable pursuits. This was different. *She* was different.

'Why would you risk being seen with me if it would damage your reputation?' Her little button nose wrinkled. 'It's just sex.'

It wasn't *just* sex. For the price of one night he would be selfish. He would claim his revenge. She had made him get attached. She had made him forget that the only person he could rely on was himself. And he hated her for that.

She was his only connection to the emotional wreck of a boy he'd been, and after their night together—after he'd shown her all he'd become, all he was now—the memory of who he'd been would be obsolete.

That rope wouldn't pull any more.

She wouldn't haunt him any more.

Because the last remaining echoes of who he had been—Akeem Ali—would be gone. That boy would be dead. Lifeless. As his father had demanded the first time they'd encountered one another.

'No one will know, *qalbi*,' he assured her. Because his people couldn't know that his primitive need to have her one last time consumed him.

He would have one night to close the doors on the past, on who he had been, so he could fully embrace his future. He would restore the monarch's reputation. He would make sure his mother's sacrifices had not been in vain.

He would have it all.

He would be King.

'You're to be a one-night stand—not my future Queen,' he finished, leaving her in no doubt of exactly where she stood in his future.

Nowhere.

It took every ounce of Charlotte's self-control not to react to the cruel sting of his confirmation. But it was as if a thousand bees had landed on her body with those words and jabbed at her exposed flesh.

One-night stand.

It didn't scream opulence. It screamed cheap and throwaway.

Her mouth ran dry. The words didn't appal her. She'd been made to feel worse. But they made her insides twist and pull.

'Get dressed, Charlotte,' Akeem ordered from the doorway when the silence sizzled, and she followed his gaze to some clothes laid on the table.

When he didn't exit the room, she jabbed a finger towards the clothes and said, 'Do you want to watch?'

Regret was instant, and it cut deep when he replied, 'Would you like me to?'

'No,' she said.

But the thought of him watching while she reached up beneath her skirt to pull down her tights…the thought of his eyes following as they skirted over her thighs, down to her knees, to land at her ankles…made her knickers damp.

Tension filled her. She didn't know what to do with her hands. They flexed and pinched together at her sides.

She turned to the bed and eyed the pattern on the bedspread. Gold. And there were gold sheets. She'd take any bet that they were actual gold— some blend, some mixture, that had softened the precious metal to his will.

She turned. 'You haven't said where it will happen. Only that it will be your bed.' Her voice pitched. 'How many beds do you have?' She arched a brow. 'Do you mean to show me all of them before we get to *the one*?'

'Many beds belong to me…in many countries. I mean to show you one bed. *My bed.* In Taliedaa.'

'I don't understand—' she started, because she didn't understand his hesitation, or her own. 'Why bring me in here, only to wait? Don't you want to do it in between gold sheets?'

Akeem screwed his face into a mask of displeasure. *'Do it?'*

'A bed is a bed. I don't understand this need of yours to wait and prolong this—especially if you don't want us to be seen.'

The click of him closing the door reverberated in the room.

'Sometimes the waiting is more pleasurable than the doing, Charlotte.' His eyes were trained on her, and he moved in, inch by inch, towards her. 'I have waited nine years for this moment and I will not rush. I will devour you with my mouth.' He stopped in front of her and her heart pounded. 'With my fingers,' he continued. 'My body will be on you. In you. I will savour you,' he promised, his voice silk. 'But only when you demand it, and not before.'

Her lungs refused to drag in air, because she knew the scent of him on her tongue, sweeping into her airways, would be fatal. She would be lost—not only to his words, but to him. Consumed by the delicious fact that he would wait.

Until *she* was ready.

The man who had abandoned her was willing to wait for her *now*. Just not when it had mattered…

She shut the thought down, because she wasn't here to confront the past, or the emotions pumping in her chest, because they scared her. They had a similarity to how he'd used to make her feel. Precious. Wanted. *Loved.* But she was here to claim her pleasure. To claim *life.* Not his love.

'Then I'm demanding it. I want it,' she said, and moved towards him, lacing her arms around his neck. 'You.'

He gently gripped the back of her neck, and the shock of his firm fingers sent little jolts of electricity through her to the depths of her stomach. 'Do you want my kisses, *qalbi?*'

She nodded, and taut, hard muscle answered her. He placed his mouth at the base of her throat, flicking his tongue in the hollow he found there.

She moaned. A tantalising pressure was building in her abdomen, and it made her press her thighs together. 'A little higher. Please…'

He moved his mouth up along the tight muscles, his teeth nibbling, his tongue caressing. His mouth closed around the flesh below her ear before he whispered, 'Always so polite, Charlotte.'

She pushed out of his embrace and he staggered, releasing her. Was she that predictable? A people-pleaser even in bed? Unexpected tears filled her eyes.

But she would not cry.

Why would she cry?

He reached for her, but she sidestepped him.

'I will not kick you out of bed for saying "please", *qalbi.*'

'What if I don't want to say it?' She bit at her

lip to stem the sting in her eyes. 'What if I don't want to be polite?'

'You have a sudden aversion to manners?'

'I have a sudden aversion to being—' she inhaled deeply and released her breath slowly, through parted lips '—predictable.'

All her life she'd done what was necessary to make others happy. To make her dad happy. Her dad had known the minute Akeem hadn't shown up nine years ago that she would stay with him. Look after him and forget everything else. Because she was *predictable*.

She closed her eyes, blocking out the gaze observing her with quiet intensity. Wasn't tonight all about her? But how could it be when she didn't know how to put herself first?

'I'm not ready,' she whispered.

Because it turned out she wasn't. Nine years he'd lived in her head. His mouth. His fingers. His touch. And now he was within reach—she was touching him. Her Akeem. Her friend. Her boyfriend. Her onetime lover.

She closed her eyes, swallowing down the sudden lump in her throat.

He wasn't *her* Akeem any more. He was the ex who'd broken her heart, and now he wanted to smooth over the cracks with something he called *closure*.

But closure didn't come from someone else, did it? Closure you had to find on your own. Or so some magazine article she'd read had said. It held true in her mind, because being in his arms—*his bed*—sounded nothing like closure. But his touch... To be touched... To find pleasure on a day when there shouldn't be pleasure...

'Then I shall wait until you are.'

His voice pulled her eyes open—pulled her back into the room and into his eyes.

He was giving her control.

'And when you are...' He moved the pad of his thumb along her cheek with a tenderness that defied the strength he radiated.

'And when I am...?' she said huskily, her insides trembling. Because she was being given the reins of something powerful—this hidden energy between them that was making her insides pull in every direction.

'It will be your choice, *qalbi*. You will lead the way and I will bring you so much pleasure.'

He rasped his promise from between open lips and she wanted to press her mouth to his. But she was afraid to lean in and capture his promise. To taste it. To take the lead.

'Rest, *qalbi*.' He released her. 'And then return to me.'

He turned his back on her, and she wilted as he closed the door behind him.

He'd pulled her from her life and thrust her into his—and she was out of her depth. But she'd got on the plane because she'd wanted to, she reminded herself. She wanted him. Wanted a moment in time she could call hers. But this wasn't her moment. It would not happen in between gold sheets because she wasn't ready and he knew it.

Keeping her clothes on, she stalked over to the bed, kicked off her shoes and ripped back the coverlet. She climbed inside, fully clothed, and pulled the golden sheets up to her chin. But something niggled at her. The way he looked at her. *Saw* her. Anticipated her needs.

No one ever did that for her. It was always her catering to everyone else. Her father... But Akeem? He'd known she needed rest before she'd admitted it to herself. He'd known she needed to control things even when she was baiting him to take her to bed.

A fatigue unlike any she'd known pulled her eyelids down despite her best efforts to keep them open.

Darkness claimed her.

CHAPTER THREE

AKEEM HAD BEEN RIGHT. She had needed to rest. But now... Now energy consumed her.

Charlotte inhaled deeply and moved her feet to bring her nose to nose with the door leading her back into the lounge. She hit the rectangular touchpad and barged her way into the room with as much confidence as she could pretend to have.

She froze on the spot. Akeem was a vision of unquestionable authority. Her eyes skimmed down the length of him. He'd changed. Gone were the western clothes and there he was in swathes of black, and a headdress with a band of gold securing it.

Her eyes moved back to his face and his clenched jaw. His eyes were moving over the dragon-green fabric covering every inch of her skin and they didn't miss a thing—from the opaque green headscarf with a gold trim that loosely covered her damp curls, to the full-length sleeves fluttering at her fingertips, the high rounded neck, and down to the flared edge of her full-length trousers.

Head high, shoulders back, she said the words she'd been practising. 'I'm ready.'

He stood, and in a single stride he was in front of her. 'Ready for what?'

She fixated on his lips. She could still feel them working along her neck. Each press of his mouth was imprinted upon her and even the shower hadn't been able to remove him…the feel of him.

She wanted those lips on her again. That was why she was here. She wanted—

'You,' she replied breathlessly.

She gasped, the throb of her heartbeat pulsing in her ears, as Akeem picked her up and brought the core of her to sit just above his. Instinctively, she wrapped her legs around his waist as firm fingers pressed into her hips. He walked with her wrapped around him like a second skin and set her down before the throne.

'What now?' she asked.

'Show me you are ready for me, *qalbi*.'

'How?'

'By removing your clothes,' he said. 'This time I want you to sit on my throne naked.'

Her chest tightened. *'Naked?'* Swallowing, she tried to ease the sudden dryness of her throat. 'I thought you wanted to wait until we were in your bed?'

The finger moving feather-light down her throat to follow the round neckline stilled. 'Are you not ready, then?'

'*I am!*'

He smiled. 'There is much I can do without claiming your body with mine,' he said, and his voice was a caress straight to the most intimate part of her.

'*Here?* Anyone could see us!'

'No one will enter without my permission.' His mouth curved in a fascinating movement, both sensual and terrifying. 'Right here, right now, you will remove your clothes.' He lifted his hands, removed his headdress, and dropped it to the floor. 'I'll go first.'

With an agile shrug he removed his robes, and pushed his boxers to his feet.

'You're naked…' she breathed, amazed at the ease with which he presented himself to her.

She couldn't help it.

She drank him in.

Every appealing curve of hard flesh.

'Does my nakedness offend you?' He stepped out of the puddle of clothes at his feet and her eyes moved down the length of him. Her mouth dried, her breath coming in sharp rasps. He was glorious. Bigger, taller—stronger than she remembered.

Her gaze stalled on the proudest part of him.

'No…' Her answer was barely audible.

She wanted to reach out and touch him the way she had nine years ago. To stroke upwards, along the hard muscles of his abdomen, to raise his T-shirt and close her mouth over a hard brown nipple.

They had been each other's first. She'd trusted him with her secrets and her body.

Did she still trust him?

Naively, she knew she did. With some false sense of security because of who they'd been. He'd offered himself to her then. Completely trusting. And he was doing it again. *Right now.* She wanted to do the same. To have the confidence of her younger self in her older body. To be as free as she had been before...*with him.*

She stood before him in front of his throne and toed off her shoes. She didn't dare to speak. She pulled her trousers down from her hips and stepped out of the clothes the way he had. She didn't dare to look away. This was life. This was *her* life. And she'd never felt as decadent or as revived as she slipped the green tunic over her head.

'Remove your bra.'

Her eyes shot back to his, and she saw his gaze was full of wild challenge.

He'd challenged her from the moment she'd walked into the pub. He'd prodded her to question why she hadn't become something *more*, understanding her doubts before she'd even given voice to them. In the car, he'd acknowledged her fears with pinpoint accuracy, and on the plane, he'd known she wasn't ready.

But he knew she was ready *now*.

He saw all the things no one had bothered to look for before. The things she'd thought were invisible. She'd thought that *she* was invisible. To her father. To the teachers she'd had in her teens, who had never recognised she was struggling. To the acquaintances in her never stable jobs. But he saw the things she'd thought no one cared to see.

Her needs.

The real her.

She slipped the bra straps from her shoulders and reached around with clumsy fingers to undo the hooks and let the fabric fall away from her breasts. Her nipples hardened into stiff peaks as he unashamedly caressed them with his eyes.

Thrilled and terrified, she hooked her fingers in the waistband of her panties.

He wanted to see her and she wanted to be seen.

By him.

He lifted his head. 'No, not those.'

Holding her breath, she stood as straight as she could wearing only her panties. 'Kiss me,' she whispered—because wasn't that what she wanted? The heat of him on her? A reminder that she was alive and really living on a day when death had been all around?

Akeem grunted and moved to capture her wrists. 'I will more than kiss you.' He drew her into his arms. 'I will devour you,' he promised, and pulled her mouth on to his.

His kiss was hungry, and she kissed him back

just as hungrily. He pushed her into the throne. The chair was cold and hard against her back, and without his heat against her she felt very naked as he kicked their clothes aside and bent to his knees before her.

'Now I taste you…' He groaned, deep in his chest. 'Kiss you where I long to most.'

Charlotte gasped as he pushed between her thighs. Her hands grabbed at him and moved onto his shoulders.

Akeem—'

His fingers pressed deep into her hipbones, holding her in place for his viewing pleasure. He didn't speak—not with words. But he spoke with his hands. His fingers slid down the arch of her hips. Soft, feather-like touches whispered along the outside of her thighs to move inwards and between her legs. Spreading her thighs wider, he bent forward and flicked his tongue against her concealed opening.

It had never been like this during their youthful relationship. Never this wild or this totally consuming. But she wanted him there, between her legs. She wanted everything. More than his kisses and his soft, yet firm tongue stroking at her slick folds. Her body screamed to feel him inside her. His fingers, his—

His mouth moved up, capturing her nub of nerves, and sucked at her through the fabric of her panties.

'Akeem!'

The surge of pleasure centred around his mouth made her cry out and arch her body into his kiss. It was an explosion of sensation. Hot and blinding. Akeem's mouth moved over her with masterful precision, sucking her deeper and deeper into his mouth. The fabric between his mouth and her core was agony personified.

But Charlotte wanted his heaviness—the length of him—inside her.

Now.

Breathless, throwing her head back, she choked out, 'My panties!' not sure if her fingers at his nape were pulling him in closer or pushing him away so he could complete the task she'd given to him so brazenly.

He moved back, and she whimpered with his absence. His thumbs hooked into the elastic at her waist and he looked up at her from his position on the ground.

'These?' he asked. He tugged gently at the elastic and let it pop back against her skin.

She flushed, the heat searing up through the valley of her breasts to slash across her cheeks as his voice, pure husky tones of desire, penetrated her more than the sting of elastic.

'Take them off,' she begged, bold and brazen and not caring one bit.

'Tell me, Lottie—what is the magic word?'

'Please!' It was a roar—a plea.

Heat and excitement spread from her toes to her tingling lips as, millimetre by agonising millimetre, he pulled them down. The stretchy lace teased her in its slow descent to her ankles. Then with open palms, he worked his way up from her knotted ankle bone back to her thighs.

She wasn't sure if the rush in her ears was because of what Akeem was doing to her or because the plane was actually tilting.

He parted her legs, hooking her ankles on the jewel-encrusted armrests. He pushed his face into the dark curls and moved his tongue in confident strokes up and down her slick core.

'Ahh...' she grunted, clawing at his shoulders, moving her hands through his hair and thrashing her body onto his face.

His tongue pushed inside her and she tightened, every muscle stretched and aching for the ping of release. His hand moved over her stomach, pushing into the pressure there. She bit her lip, clamping down as his thumb moved rhythmically over her core and his tongue continued to penetrate her.

Her legs squirmed on the armrests but he kept her legs pinned open with his lips clamped to her core. Charlotte's control shattered, explosions taking off deep in her abdomen. The plane bounced hard, again and again, but the bounce seemed in sync with her body so she ignored it.

The earth was actually moving.

The orgasm ripping through her was unlike any other, and for a moment she was lost.

Akeem planted a kiss to her pulsing core and whispered, 'Now every time you say *please* you will see my face.'

She opened one eye and stared down at him. His face between her thighs was a surreal reality as she came back down to earth.

He smiled. 'We have arrived, *qalbi.*'

She winced as she tried to unhook her ankles, and Akeem reached for her. His palms, gentle but firm, closed around her ankles and lowered them for her, placing her feet carefully on the floor.

His eyes burned with glistening need and she felt...decadent.

Alive.

Anything but predictable.

'Please...' She smiled down at him, trying the word for size, and his face was all she could see. 'I want more.'

'More?' His mouth tilted into a crocked smile. 'There will be plenty of time for more.'

She stilled as he stood between her legs, proud and open in his desire for her. Her instinct was to reach for him and pull him down to her. Make him beg for the release he'd given her with his hands.

His mouth...

She wanted to use her mouth too. To taste him as she never had. To pull his ecstasy from him until he murmured *please* again and again as his hands wound into her hair.

'Does pleasure make you bold?' he asked.

Raising her eyes, she met his. Not only was he looking at her. *Seeing* her. He was acting on what he saw and she didn't know how to feel about that. No one had ever done it before. Put her needs first. Not even him. Their plan to elope—to run away—had been about them both. But now...? This moment...? It was all about her. Her pleasure.

Slowly, she took him in. Akeem... The power of his attraction to her gave her wings. Confidence. Allowed her to sit there on an actual throne—naked—without the urge to hide a single blemish.

Why *was* that?

Her heart thumped. Because she wasn't invisible. Here—now—in his eyes she was everything.

She felt empowered. Strong. *Bold.*

'Yes,' she replied.

The desire pulsing between her legs made her reach for him. For the erection she wanted to feel in her hands. It was his turn. She wanted to make him throb as she had. With her mouth.

He caught her wrist. 'I will enjoy you being bold.' He placed her hand, palm down, on his abdomen, and she splayed her fingers beneath his. 'But not yet.'

With his hand guiding hers, her fingers travelled up the firm lines of his stomach to his chest,

and traced through the soft fuzz of dark hair. So
soft. So hard. So surreal…

This wasn't real.

Alone—*here*—they were *this*.

She was this.

Different.

It would be all too easy to let herself keep falling. To fall into the heat of him again and again—
to stay wrapped in the tingles of ecstasy. Forget
who he was. Forget herself. Who *she* was. Only
allow herself to remember the pleasure. This
Charlotte felt visible. *Powerful*.

'Pleasure made me forget,' she said, reminding
herself that just because she'd forgotten, it didn't
mean the outside world didn't exist.

'Forget what?'

'Everything,' she whispered honestly, his gaze
leaving her no room to mask her features from her
thoughts. She dipped her chin to her chest. Breaking the agonising intensity of his eyes.

'Everything?' He pressed his hand down on
hers and pushed her palm into him. Into the hot-
ness of him. The hardness. 'Or,' he continued,
eyes narrowed, 'have you only forgotten the parts
that do not matter here?'

'But they do matter, don't they? Because when
I go home it will all still be there.'

You won't, she finished silently.

But the grief? The regret? They'd still be there.
A bubble surrounded them, she realised. A mist

of pleasure was wrapped around them, holding them suspended in time. *Together.* But after their one night they'd never be together again.

He shrugged, releasing her, and she watched as he walked to one of the sofas and tore free one of the golden throws.

Walking back towards her, he shook out the blanket and went on bended knee to cover her nakedness with smooth silk. The fabric imprisoned the ends of her hair and puffed it around her face. Akeem slipped his hands behind her back and pulled free the trapped hair until it fell about her shoulders and down to her chest in long, winding curls.

'If it will still be there, why not allow yourself pleasure unreservedly? Permit me to make you forget, again and again. What waits for you no longer matters until it matters.'

For twenty-four hours surely she could let herself go? Why not let herself float as high as she could in his embrace, locked inside a bubble of make-believe?

But if she let herself float too far—too high—and he popped it before she could...left her again... Unprepared...

This time, would she recover?

She had to pop it. The bubble. She needed to shield herself from the influence of the pleasure Akeem could give to her. From the power of it.

'You made me forget before,' she said, the memory claiming her, 'but not with your body.'

Dark eyes snapped to hers. 'No,' he agreed. 'It was with my tongue.'

'At St John's,' she clarified.

It was a happy memory. She didn't have many. The bad often took over whatever good there had been. But she wanted to remember this.

She wanted *him* to remember.

'You let me draw you, again and again, until I got it right,' she reminded him, and sucked them both into the shared memory of sitting under a huge tree in the children's home garden.

He'd given her an escape from reality by simply offering his body—his presence—and she'd longed to stay there, under the oak tree, with her pencils and paper.

With Akeem...

Maybe for twenty-four hours she could stay with him again? But this time she would protect herself with the knowledge that the fairy tale would end, and then her reality could be whatever she wanted it to be. Hers.

Pulling her hand free from beneath his, she lifted it to his cheek. 'I'd like to draw you again,' she whispered, moving her thumb along his jaw, stroking it through the bristles of his short beard until she came to his mouth. A mouth she had drawn many times during their shared time in care.

It had been nearly ten years since she'd picked

up a pencil. Since her father had destroyed all her portraits of Akeem.

The only memories she'd had of him—or of her dreams—were in her head, but drawing this newer, older Akeem would be a reminder of who she had been before. Of the dreams she'd tentatively told him about, of being a professional artist, until her father had reminded her it that she hadn't got time to dream.

Akeem had helped her to forget who she was once. Maybe this time he could help her remember who she wanted to be. Who she might become when this day was over.

She could still draw.

She could still dream.

There was nothing stopping her now.

Only herself.

Three sharp raps on the door and the sound of the double doors opening broke the moment between them.

Akeem spat out a word she didn't understand, but it set her nerves on edge and halted the footsteps of whoever was entering.

Charlotte tried to make a sound of protest—she was naked under the blanket—but with a small shake of his head he silenced her, his eyes wide, his jaw clenched…

She was in the presence of a king and not a lover now.

The bubble had popped, hadn't it?

And she wasn't ready—she wasn't prepared.

Her fingers poked through the blanket to grip onto her makeshift lapels, and she tugged the silk tighter around her shoulders.

'Do not enter,' Akeem commanded.

His voice was now controlled, and even. Focused and sure, his dark gaze stayed on hers. Her breathing sped up and she opened her mouth to speak, but before she could form the words his lips pressed against hers.

A feather-light touch of his mouth.

It was a promise.

His promise.

He stood, and it wasn't the fear of facing reality that she wasn't prepared for, and it wasn't whoever had started to come through the door that scared her, nor was it the embarrassment threatening to undo her that she'd been caught naked, wrapped around the son of a king.

It was him.

Covering her nakedness before his own. Not with the blanket but with his body. Big and wide, he shielded her, doing what no one else ever had. Protecting her.

He turned and walked towards the obscured glass double doors, towards whoever had been about to walk through the door, and continued to block her view with his physique.

His nakedness was its own flawless armour, she realised. It wasn't a handmade suit or the robes of a prince he required, but only his skin. Only the man had to be present. Because even without expensive fabrics, he still exuded the power only the son of a king could.

An unexpected thrill burned through her, catching her breath in her throat—because whoever was coming through those doors, a king protected her.

He'd made a mistake.

Scandal.

The word pulled at his insides, threatening to break the rigid control straightening his shoulders.

He could not hide her.

The skeleton crew he'd travelled with to England was all for nothing.

The moment those doors opened Charlotte would no longer be his secret, because there in front of him stood his royal guard and two of his most senior aides.

His men.

On arrival in Taliedaa, the moment the wheels touched the ground, his men would be ready to protect their new King. And here they were, ready—because it was their job to seek him out and assure themselves of his safety.

He'd forgotten.

In a single undeniable moment he'd become more than his father's son in his men's eyes. He had become his father. Because he'd taken his pleasure in the most abandoned way and forgotten himself.

A confident man often did things out of the ordinary without anxiety. But a king? He could do what he liked.

But not the kind of king he needed to become. The embodiment of control.

His gut clenched. He would not follow his instinct and tell his men to get out again, because his men deserved the respect his father hadn't ever shown them. The respect his father demanded himself, although he hadn't deserved it.

He'd expected everyone else to be everything he wasn't.

His father had been a king of contradictions.

Nine years he'd spent, proving he was neither his father's son, nor the boy who'd arrived in Taliedaa. Because the Crown Prince made his choices based on the price of his actions.

Another lesson his father had taught him quickly.

He, the orphan heir, next in line to succeed to the throne, was stronger than his father. Better not because of him, but despite him. His father's reign of pleasure-seeking at the price of the crown's reputation—at the cost of his mother's reputation—was over.

Akeem's chest heaved as his men's narrowed eyes tried to see past him. To see *her*. He stepped forward, one step at a time, backing them up and away from the door. Blocking their view.

'Your Highness…' The head of his royal guard had the good grace to blush, and the three men behind him bowed their heads.

'Are my people well?' Akeem asked.

His bow deepened in response to the silent reprimand. 'Yes…' he answered, and then raised his gaze questioningly to Akeem's.

Akeem cocked a brow. 'Does the palace still stand?'

'Yes, it is as you left it.'

'Does the sun still set?'

'Within the hour, Your Royal Highness.'

'All is as it should be, then?'

Eyes as dark as his own widened as they glanced down at his nakedness. 'Yes,' he answered, the blush tingeing his cheeks turning from a slight pink to a deep red.

Akeem tutted his disapproval, but he felt his insides snake around his lungs and squeeze. He could not deny or explain what had taken place in the room behind him without making the situation worse.

Immediately, his path became clear. As it had when he'd been eighteen and thrown into his father's world.

He would not be *him*. His men deserved more, and so did his people. He would prove that the illegitimate Crown Prince was worthy to be their

King. Worthy of the crown. And there was only one way to do it—to keep his reputation intact and make his people believe that he would never give in to his baser instincts like his father.

The scene behind him was not the beginning of the end of his new reign. It was not a replay of his father taking his pleasure without decency or care—

Isn't it?

No!

Why not?

Because…

He couldn't answer.

In his men's eyes, it *was* a replay. A descent into his father's kind of chaos. In this moment he was just as bad as his father, ordering his men to stay and watch as women pleasured him.

He ground his teeth.

He would fix this.

He made himself stalk closer to his men, and with his voice low and sure he said, 'Imagine interrupting the King and your future Queen simply to tell him the sky is indeed blue…'

Tension radiated from every taut line of his royal guard's body. 'Your Royal Highness—'

Akeem shook his head and halted the stumbling apology with a lazy flick of his wrist.

'The helicopter,' he commanded. 'Fifteen minutes.'

Akeem hit the button, sealing the doors on his

fate. He closed his eyes. A decade of ignoring his feelings—his urges—and for what? To risk it all? Jaw rigid, he looked at her then. *For her?*

She stood, her hair a crown of curls, trailing down her bare shoulders to fall over her breasts, and her skin shimmered as iridescently as the jewels surrounding her.

'Are you okay?' she asked.

His heart galloped into a frenzied beat. 'Am *I* okay?'

'Are you?'

Was he? He couldn't remember the last time anyone had asked. His feelings didn't matter. Only his blood. Only his duty.

He nodded, but his heart refused to stop its treacherous double beat as she moved towards him.

'The one thing you didn't want to happen…'

She stopped in front of him, the scent of her dragging over his senses. What scent? What power did she possess to make a king become only a man before her? To make him revert to his most basic self?

'And now it's happened.'

She gasped as the blanket slipped from her shoulders. Akeem caught the falling fabric on instinct, and for a moment everything stilled as her nakedness beneath revealed itself.

He moved quickly, trying not to absorb the sight of her—her skin, her curves—trying not to remember what she'd felt like beneath his fingertips. He took her hand, ignoring the heat of her palm, and thrust the fabric into it. She wrapped the blanket under her arms and tucked it between her breasts.

Her cheeks high in colour, she asked, 'Does it matter that they caught us? That we—you—?' She stuttered and shook her head, her crown of curls bouncing on her shoulders.

'Yes,' he said, feeling low embers of the fire they'd shared threatening to burst into flame. He would ignore it—as he should have until he had her firmly in his bed, between his thighs. But still he couldn't resist, and continued, 'It matters that I made you come apart with my mouth.'

Her hand paused in tucking in her makeshift tunic. *'Exactly!'* she replied,

But he heard the quiver in her breath as she remembered. Remembered his mouth on her. Tasting her.

She crouched down with her back to him to pick up their discarded clothes. 'I don't have a clue what's happening, or what you're feeling—'

'Feelings have no place here.'

Clothes in hand, she turned to face him. 'Who told you that?'

Every muscle in his naked body turned taut, from the tendons in his toes flattening his feet against the plush carpeted floor to the muscles elongating his throat. 'The crown must come before feelings or emotion,' he rasped deeply. 'One must obey one's duty first.'

The stab of those teachings still cut deep.

And now Charlotte Hegarty had unpicked the adhesive holding his life together and bared the truth. One misstep had been all it took to reveal that he was still reactive to his primitive urges. *Weak.*

The silken touch of her hand on his jolted him straight back into the room. Her small delicate fingers held out his robes to him.

'So they saw me?' she asked.

In the eyes of his men today he was like his father. But if he did what his father had not… If he married her. Made her his Queen. The *people's* Queen…

There was no other choice.

He snatched the robe from her and thrust his arms inside. 'They saw no one but me,' he said, because they hadn't. But they'd seen enough. The unmistakable truth…

'But you were naked—'

'Very.'

'So was I…underneath this.' The green of her eyes, bright with questions, searched his. 'Thank you for hiding me. Whether it was for you or for me…' She shrugged. 'I'm grateful you didn't let them see me fully.'

'Do not thank me yet.'

In a single stride he was on her. In her breathing

space. Close enough to be reminded of how sweet the musk was lingering on her skin and in the air. On his lips—his tongue. To be reminded of how desire had changed the game and now it was no longer a game of revenge—of getting even. But a game of duty.

'You may not like what comes next,' he said, capturing her waist in his palms and scooping her over his shoulder.

'Akeem!'

The weight of her over his shoulder and her perfectly pert bottom in his eyeline sent a rush of lava through his veins. The temptation to take her to bed returned.

He'd given himself a reprieve—a moment to think and save Charlotte from any embarrassment. But the truth was undeniable. He'd been caught behaving like his father, and he wouldn't allow himself—his reputation—to be so vulnerable again.

She swivelled on his shoulder. 'What are you doing?'

He moved towards the exit. 'I'm taking you back to your room.'

'To my room?' Her fingers pinched into his shoulders as he exited the lounge. 'You can't dismiss me and send me to my room because you don't like what I'm saying. I have a right to know what happens next—'

Thrusting open the suite door, he stalked towards the bed and lowered her onto the edge of the mattress. 'Get dressed and wait for me.'

He turned, pushing from his mind the image of a naked Charlotte waiting for him on this bed. It tugged at him…the idle notion of wishing he could be a man—nothing more than primitive need—and finishing what they'd started and finding ignorance in her body.

But he wasn't just a man. He was the son of a king. A crown prince. A crown prince who had surrendered to his baser instincts and proved his father right.

'I don't understand,' Charlotte called after him.

He couldn't say what made him stop. What made him turn around. But he did. And the sight of her—vulnerable and confused—almost broke him. *He'd* done that to her. Taken his pleasure and thrown her into a world so unlike her own.

He closed his eyes. 'Please, *qalbi*,' he said, because he was not averse to the word. He knew the power of it, and he saw it in her eyes and in her silence as she recognised his need for her to obey. As he had obeyed her. He had torn those panties straight from her body to give her the release she craved.

Yet his was a different plea.

He needed a moment to reconcile himself to what was to happen. What he *had* to do to be the King he'd spent almost a decade becoming.

He opened his eyes. 'You're not meant to understand,' he said, 'but you will.'

'When?'

'Soon,' he promised. 'Get dressed and wait for me.'

Closing the door behind him, he moved towards his own suite with an ease he didn't feel.

He'd demanded his night of revenge, and he'd been so close to victory.

But at what cost?

CHAPTER FOUR

HER WHOLE LIFE she'd been waiting for other people. For her dad to return home safely, before his nightly blackout occurred. And then for Akeem. She'd waited for him before...only to be given a firm reminder never to rely on anyone but herself.

Akeem hadn't bothered to turn up back then— because why would he? He'd got what he'd wanted. Her surrender. Her body. And then *whoosh*. He'd been gone. And that had been that until he'd wanted something...

She pulled the tunic top over her head and thrust her arms into the full sleeves, then bent to pull her underwear on. The dampness of Akeem's kisses still clung to her panties, making her pause and making her heart hammer. She picked up the trousers and pushed her toes in with force.

All the relationships she'd known had been *take, take, take*, and that was why she'd never give her heart again. Ever. Because she had nothing left to give. To anyone. Maybe not even to herself.

She'd wanted a night—one night—when her

needs came first. *Hers.* And look where her stupid desire to be selfish had led her.

She wanted to go home.

She was done with waiting. Done with the promise of *soon.* Life was now, wasn't it?

Opening the bedroom door, she looked down the long corridor with doors on either side. Was that a staircase?

She moved towards it and grabbed the balustrade. Her bare feet connected to a smooth surface resembling reflective glass, and she descended to be met with another lounge of sorts. More beige sofas sat parallel to the staircase that spiralled into the room, reclining chairs, TVs, and—

Subtle vibrations teased her bare toes, and she flexed them against the smooth veneered floor. The vibrations got heavier, pulsing at her insides. There was a door in the middle of the floating staircase. And the white column descending through the middle was a…a *lift.*

It was!

The white lift's doors slid open slowly—the polar opposite to her pumping heart. Holding her breath, she stood rooted.

'Why are you hiding down here?'

Dressed and unruffled, Akeem appeared before her. Perfectly perfect in every way.

Something inside her snapped.

Caring for her dad had taught her to listen first

and react later—*in private*—but not now. She wouldn't wait. She wouldn't hold back.

She couldn't.

She was going to cut herself loose from the control she'd so carefully maintained to keep her standing every time her dad lashed out or berated her for simply *being*.

She stirred her legs into motion, moving towards him with purpose. Her body was unstoppable as it realised its aim. It was thrilling—intoxicating. *Surreal*. Her stomach muscles hardened. She'd never felt so calm and yet enraged before.

Charlotte raised her arm, closing her fingers together to create as much surface area as possible on her open palm, and—

Akeem caught her wrist in mid-air. 'You will not strike the King.'

'I'm not striking the King,' she hissed, the pressure of her raised arm keeping her face only millimetres from his mouth. 'I'm about to slap you—the man. Not the King with golden sheets and an aeroplane bigger than a high-rise flat. *You*.'

'The truth is always hard to hear, but they are one and the same.' He pinned her wrists and raised them to the sides of head, then moved in until they were nose to nose. 'Striking me is an arrestable offence.'

'Why break a habit of a decade?' she spat between tight lips. 'Why not take me to the police station right now and leave me to fend for myself, the way you've always done.'

He recoiled, breaking the contact of their over-sensitised bodies. 'I have never left you,' he corrected, his nostrils flaring as he half turned his body away from her.

She laughed, a hiccup of a sound, as she pushed herself free from the cold metal at her back. 'You just did!' She raised her hands and dropped them with a smack to her thighs when he didn't respond. 'Take me home, Akeem.' It was a hushed plea. 'Now.'

'You can't leave.'

'Why? Does the plane need fuel?'

He shook his head. 'No.'

'Then why not?' she asked, eyebrows high. 'You're the King. Make it happen.'

'I am not King yet, *qalbi*.'

'What does that mean?'

'How they found us…saw me…' He inhaled deeply, his shoulders widening as he seemed to grow bigger—taller. 'It was in a moment when I forgot my duty and became what I fear most.'

'Like your dad?'

He opened his mouth only a fraction, and she watched as his lips moved without sound. His lips thinned, and he nodded. 'Their catching us together will reinforce the doubt my people have. They think my rule will follow in his footsteps.

That just like him my needs will come before my country.'

'Aren't they right?' she asked, before she could stop herself. 'You wanted to hide me—sneak me in and out of your bed—just to fulfil your needs.'

'I know what I did.'

'Why did you do it?' she asked.

His eyes held fast to hers. 'I couldn't help myself.'

'Neither could I,' she whispered. 'But that doesn't tell me why.'

'Can *you* explain what happened?' he asked. 'The intensity?'

Could she? Nine years had passed between them—it seemed like a lifetime but still…no, she couldn't.

'But if you didn't want to be seen with me…' Her stomach muscles tightened. He didn't want to be seen with the daughter of an alcoholic, did he? A nobody. She wasn't his future Queen—she was a mistake. But she needed to know why he'd taken such a risk. She hadn't asked before—she'd been too focused on her own reasons. Her own need to put the past behind her. 'Why did you put yourself in such a vulnerable position to be caught in the first place, when it was the last thing you wanted to happen?'

'My father had a lifetime of being reckless for his own amusement—'

'And you wanted a taste of it?'

'No,' he denied, his voice a harsh rasp.

'Then what *did* you want?' she pushed.

'A night—'

'You risked your reputation for a night?' She cut him off, her insides twisting. 'We haven't even made it to your bed.' She blew out a puff of agitated air. 'Not *your* bed. Not the only bed you deem fit for purpose.'

'Make no mistake,' he warned. 'Things have changed.'

'Changed?'

'My bed is off-limits.'

She laughed, a throaty gurgle. 'How dare you pull me from my life, fly me who knows how many miles into a kingdom I've never heard of and then turn the tables on me?' She fixed him with an exasperated glare.

'If the tables have turned on anyone,' he replied, 'it is me. Because you will be my wife.'

'Wife!' she scoffed. Old hurts bloomed fast, and his cruel joke hurt more than it should. 'I'm a one-night stand,' she reminded him. 'Not your future Queen.'

She exhaled heavily, forcing herself to blow out all the heaviness in her chest. In her heart.

'I'm done with this game,' she said, steeling herself to the truth. This was over before it had begun. He was a prince, and she was the daughter of Damien Hegarty. It was in her genes to fail. 'I don't belong here. Send me home, Akeem.'

'It's too late for that,' he said, and a deep flush stained his cheeks. 'There is only one solution and your leaving is not it.'

Her gut dropped to her toes. 'Solution?'

'When you leave this plane you will enter my kingdom as its future Queen.'

Her mouth open, she stared at him. He hadn't been playing with her.

He nodded—a small inclination of his head.

'They could have caught you with anyone...'

'But you aren't anyone.'

'No, I'm not,' she agreed, 'but I could have been. Would you have married someone else?'

'No.'

'Why not?'

'Because there has only ever been you, *qalbi.*'

'*What?*' she asked. 'What about no one ever complaining about your stamina? What about you being more skilled than the boy I remember? You're lying,' she accused, her cheeks tight with tension. 'Why would you lie?'

'No one has ever complained because no one has ever been in my bed besides me. The boy you remember had no control—he was a boy. I am a man. I have control in more ways than one,' he told her. 'And I do not lie.'

'If the only person you've ever been with is me, how could you possibly know that you could give me extreme pleasure?' she pushed, trying to catch him out in his unnecessary lie.

Why was he doing it? Telling her it had only ever been her. To persuade her to say yes? To get her to marry him? It wasn't her destiny to be a queen. If her dad had been right, she was only ever destined to fail. And he *had* been right, hadn't he? The one time he'd needed her she hadn't been there. The idea of her being a queen... *Ridiculous!*

'You couldn't,' she answered for him, because his lies would not convince her to say yes to being his wife when he didn't want her in his bed. Let alone his life! 'Then why...?' She searched for the right words, but she didn't have any. She knew why *she* hadn't been with anyone else. But him? The son of a king had denied himself. It made no sense.

'Because the only thing that matters here is my duty,' he answered. 'My people need stability. Not a king who puts his pleasure first—'

'But today—'

'I made a mistake.'

She furrowed her brow. 'Is that why you wanted me here? In your bed?' she asked, her gut twisting. 'Because I represent a life you can't have—?' She cut herself off as an acrid taste flooded her mouth.

'Yes. That is exactly why I wanted you in my bed, *qalbi*. Because I knew when you left it— when our night was over—the past and the boy you knew would be gone. For ever.'

'That makes no sense!' she screeched.

'It doesn't have to make sense to you.'

But it did!

She wanted to wail, but she folded her arms around her chest, felt the thud of her heart pounding against her palm. He was right. It didn't have to make sense. She was here. *They* were here.

'Our marriage,' he continued, dismissing her line of questioning, 'will show my people I am stable. Grounded. I will be secure in my role as King in the eyes of my men. My people.'

'And you think by making *me* your wife—their Queen—is the stability they need?' Raising her chin, she asked, 'But what about my life? I can't just up sticks and—'

'As we have already established, there is nothing at home for you.'

No, he'd established that she had no job, and soon she'd have no home. They hadn't talked about her non-existent friends, or how empty her life was now she didn't have to care for her dad. But what about her dreams? There was nothing holding her back any more.

She could have been anything... She still could be...

'I have plans. I'm going to college,' she told him, revealing her plans to them both before she'd thought them through. 'I'm going to enrol as soon as the college announces the new intake date and I'm going to get my Visual Arts diploma.'

'And your tuition fees?' Smooth as silk, he sliced through the rebirth of her old dream.

Money, time and her dad had always been the excuses for why she couldn't chase her dreams before. Why she couldn't go to college. Why she couldn't take her talent and do something with it. Now her dad was gone, and time was all she had. But money…?

'I'll find a way. A job. Something permanent.' She'd never had a permanent job before. Her dad had always made it difficult, and part-time work had been the only option.

At her last job—the call centre—she'd been on the phone to her boss once, about adding more shifts to her rota, and her dad had been screaming curse words in the background about something… a poor bet. And of course it had been her fault he'd lost. Her boss had told her not to come back.

But she didn't have to worry about her dad any more—not the poor bets, or the drinking binges he'd thought he deserved for losing, or putting him back together when he'd been full of regret.

It was just her now.

'I saw a vacancy at the local primary school before you kidnapped me from my life—for an assistant to work in early years education. Creative sessions…'

She frowned, trying to recall what the role had actually been and why it had lingered in her memory. She hadn't thought it was possible before. Her getting a job at a school. She'd barely made it through school herself. But that had changed.

'It was in art.' The words exploded from her mouth. The vacancy had stayed with her because it was about *art*. Her dream. 'Messy play for children with additional educational needs. I like kids—'

'When have *you* come into contact with children?'

'Christmas work in retail,' she explained. 'Kids get bored when their parents are shopping. I talked to them.'

By accident, she'd learnt that children responded when spoken to like human beings. And it had always filled her with a sense of pride when one of the mums juggling more than one child had appreciated her intervention. She could work with children. *She could!* She'd combine her love of art and kids while working on her portfolio as a portrait artist.

She'd always wanted to be an artist. Her heart raced. She still could be.

Her face hardened as Akeem's lips parted to flash a gleam of perfectly white teeth.

'Are you laughing at me?' she asked. Because how many times had she been laughed at in school? Called stupid for drawing nudes? For recreating the pictures she'd coveted in art books well past their due date back in the library?

Wincing, she felt memories catch her between the eyes. How hard her father had laughed when he'd found her portraits. When she'd told him about becoming a professional portraitist. When Akeem had left her behind and she'd confessed she'd attended a taster session for a diploma in Visual Arts at the local college?

He'd hidden all her art supplies then. Destroyed her work. Her memories. But she'd still had her books. He hadn't taken those, and she'd devoured them. Repeatedly. Lost in fantasy, in fairy tale and romance.

'No, I am smiling at your ability to surprise me. I would never laugh at your dreams.'

She gritted her teeth and tried to dismiss the response her body was having to his obvious sincerity.

'You can do your diploma here,' he said.

'Here?'

'Why not here?' he countered. 'I can fly in a professor of the arts to give you one-to-one tutoring. You'd get your diploma, Charlotte.'

She could get her diploma…

What choice did she have, anyway? There was nothing at home for her, but here she wouldn't be standing still any more. She could start walking towards her dreams. Towards claiming back her identity with her art.

She could make a life to call her own.

But what kind of life would it be?

A restricted life.

A life where her husband locked his bedroom door in the name of duty.

She understood why he'd said it—that his bed was off-limits. But she could still feel it. The energy between them. The knowledge that in an instant they could both be naked and in the same situation they'd been in upstairs.

The attraction between them was powerful. She'd be a fool to deny it. But a sexless and loveless marriage sounded...*painful.* Emotionally. Mentally.

Was she strong enough to agree to be his Queen—to help him build a secure reputation as King—while forging forward and making her own life? If she left—went home—would she regret that she had never seized the opportunity? Squeezed every ounce of opportunity from it for herself?

Opportunity was to be had if she let herself. If she closed her heart to the people they'd been and accepted the people they were now.

And who were they?

He was a king, and she...

She was going to be selfish, wasn't she? *Bold.* Live her life.

But a night of sex and marriage were two different things. If she closed herself off to the emotions raging inside her chest—if she didn't let him in—she could be the Queen he needed *and* get her diploma.

Couldn't she?

Was he even giving her a choice?

She inhaled deeply and nodded. 'I'll do it,' she agreed with a firm, confident nod. 'I'll marry you.'

'For the price of a diploma you'd accept the consequences of our actions…?'

Akeem sucked in a lungful of air. He didn't get angry any more. He stayed in control of all things. At all times. But the thought that Charlotte would concede to his demand just so that she could get her diploma made him angry.

He alone wasn't enough. He, as a man, would never be enough. Not for his father. Not for *her*. He was an afterthought, a consequence, a burden she would have to carry—as he always had been. He'd only ever been wanted when he had something to give.

His blood.

A diploma…

The wildfire of her eyes met his. 'Of course not.'

Her denial sent the pent-up rage blooming inside him straight to the surface of his skin. His time in care came back to him. Foster home after foster home…surrounded by family and constantly being an outsider. Unwanted, but endured for the cheque at the end of the month.

Until Charlotte.

Until she'd wrapped him up in her lies and promises to do more than endure him, to love him. And in the end she'd rejected him too, because he hadn't offered her enough. Escape with him hadn't been enough when he'd been nothing more than an orphan, working his way up on a construction site.

He held his breath. His feeling on discovering he was a prince, needed but not wanted, and definitely not *loved*, returned with a tug and a twist to his innards.

He'd tested her back then by not telling her his secret, and she'd failed him like all the others. And she'd failed him again now. Because now she wanted what he could offer.

He focused hard on the woman before him. He needed to hear it. Needed her to confess. He moved towards her and she backed up against the wall.

'If I had told you nine years ago I was a prince,' he started, and placed his palms on either side of her head as he leant in, 'would my crown have brought your loyalty? Would you have made a different choice, *qalbi*?'

'What do you mean?' she asked.

The scent of her filled him, goading him to react to the betrayal that lingered in his soul rather than do what he should do and keep his distance from her, control himself. He could still taste the sweetness of her centre in his mouth, feel her orgasm ripping through her as he'd—

Dark brows rose above her narrowed eyes. 'I

waited and you never showed up. That wasn't a choice.'

His fingers, gentle but firm, gripped her chin. 'Lies…'

She splayed her hands beneath his. 'Oh, how hard it must be for you to remember that day you promised to meet my dad now you are the *mighty* Prince Akeem.' She shook her head. 'My dad was actually really great about meeting you. He was really excited. He sent me out to get some nice bits in—'

'Nice bits?' he squawked, his dark eyes widening.

'Biscuits, cake…' She shrugged. 'I'd brought no one home before. Well, not through the front door.'

Her eyes flashed, and he remembered too. Sneaking in through her bedroom window to hide from the drunken rants downstairs. Holding her until silence filled the darkness. How he'd sworn he would never leave her alone in the dark again.

'He was never sober enough,' she added, slicing through his memory. 'But I had no real friends. Friends who would understand that just because my dad was *him*, he wasn't *me*. It was special, my bringing you to meet him, and he saw that.' She sighed. 'When I came back from the shop we waited together, with my suitcase, but you forgot all about me—Crown Prince Akeem.'

'I have forgotten nothing.'

He released her, because the confident thrust of her chin bit at him. He'd been confident too. *Once.* He'd walked step by step through the garden gate hanging by one hinge, up the overgrown path to her front door, and he had knocked with the confidence of a man coming to claim his love. To save it. To cherish it. To protect it.

But love hadn't been there.

Love had not conquered all.

Love was a lie and she was a liar.

'How convenient that you have forgotten about the text message in your recap of events.'

'The text message?' Her eyes widened. 'What text?'

What text?

His hands fisted at his sides as he fought the urge to touch her and demand the truth. The truth she denied. The truth he'd denied too, until his phone had vibrated in his back pocket and the text message had proved every word her father had said had come from *her* mouth.

The mouth he had kissed.

The mouth he'd watched speak his name again and again as he'd thrust inside her.

The mouth that had claimed his as he'd driven them both to a shared orgasm. Their first together. As one. They'd been born again, promising one another. To be together. To be married. To be a family.

All lies!

'The text message,' he growled, 'from your phone.'

'What did it say?'

'You know what it said—you sent it.'

She looked him dead in the eyes. 'I never sent you a message.'

Had she forgotten? Had he been so easy to forget? Only to be remembered when he had something to give her?

'How dare you stand there and lie?' he hissed between gritted teeth. He'd accused her dad of lying. Called him a drunken fool and told him that *his* Charlotte would say no such thing.

She was honest.

Kind.

But she'd toyed with him.

She'd made him believe he was wanted.

She'd made him get attached.

She'd made him weak.

The amber specks in her right iris blazed. 'What did the message say?'

My dad needs me. I'm not coming with you. I never was.

Verbatim, he said those three brief sentences out loud.

What a fool he'd been to believe she wanted him. No one had ever wanted him. Not his father. Not Charlotte. People only wanted what he could offer them. His blood. His time. His sacrifice.

At eighteen years of age he'd promised himself they'd rejected him for the last time. He would make himself better. Stronger. And not only would he be needed, *they* would want him. *Need him.*

What boy of eighteen would have taken the other option? Returned to his former life as a no one? A life that didn't need or want him?

Here, he had power. Here, he had choices. Here, he was the protector of his people. Duty-bound to his country. And now his duty bound him to the past, because he'd been reckless enough to flaunt it in his present.

His mistake had bound him to Charlotte.

His little liar.

'I didn't send that message,' she said.

Raising her arms, he laced them around his neck and pulled her to him, into his hardness.

'I will seduce you right here and now as an incentive to tell the truth,' he proclaimed.

He would kiss her until her bones melted. Until she didn't know where she started and he began.

'I am telling the truth!'

Her words shook him out of his angry haze and he exhaled fully, leaving his chest empty. He was drained. Mentally. Physically.

What was she doing to him? To his control?

'You left me alone to explain myself to your father,' he accused, all too aware of the memory of how he'd stood his ground for both of them. For Charlotte. Until she'd texted him with the truth. Her own words—typed by her own fingers. 'You couldn't be bothered to face me yourself and tell me you weren't coming with me. You left your drunken excuse of a father and a text to do your dirty work.'

'But I... You never came...'

He ignored her. 'Do you know what he called me?'

'What did he call you?' Her voice was so quiet...so timid.

'He called me a monster for wanting you by my side.' Damien Hegarty had called him much worse, but he would not repeat those words—he would not hear them again. He'd been called many things throughout his childhood: withdrawn, unwanted, a bastard. But a monster? And the other sickening words he'd called him? Only once.

What about your Father, Akeem? He called you much worse.

This wasn't about his father.

Isn't it?

He pushed the voice aside. No, it was firmly about *her*.

'I was newly eighteen,' he continued. 'You were sixteen. He said he'd told you about men like me who use young girls and then throw them away. Rotten men. Broken men. He was glad you had used me for your own enjoyment.'

He couldn't stop, even though everything in him told him to calm down. To breathe. To let it go. But he hadn't been able to let it go—let *her go*—for nine years, and it had brought him nothing but chaos.

'He said you were not as naïve as you'd made out. That you'd wanted a good time and used me to achieve it. You'd prearranged my meeting with your dad to make sure I got the message that you never wanted to see me again. And then my mobile phone pinged with a text to confirm everything he'd told me.'

'And you believed him?' she husked, her chest rising and falling as rapidly as his heart was pumping. 'After everything?' She paled. 'You believed everything my father told you?'

Her voice was quiet, but every word boomed through him like a bass drum.

Pinching the bridge of her nose, she pushed out a slow, deep breath. 'After everything we'd shared, you walked away because you believed I'd tricked you? Because my dad said so?' She released the bridge of her nose and turned her attention to him. 'Then you didn't really know me at all.'

'I believed the message that came from your phone and told me you weren't coming.'

And he had believed it. Why wouldn't he when it had been from her phone? Why wouldn't he believe she'd written it when throughout his life his caregivers had all written little notes in their brown manila files, explaining why yet again he couldn't remain with the family he'd been housed with?

'Told me you had no intention of coming with me.'

Her intense, stony stare held him captive. 'It wasn't me.'

'He betrayed you?' The question was out before he could digest it.

'My dad…' She gave a half-hearted shrug. 'He was a villain, wasn't he?' A weak smile tormented her lips. 'He used our own vulnerabilities against us. He trapped me into thinking he was all I had, and he convinced you I didn't want you any more.'

'It's not true,' he whispered—because it couldn't be. Damien had not cheated him.

'I didn't have my phone. My dad knew you were coming and he sent me out of the house,' she recapped, her breathing quickening into short little rasps. 'It is the truth. I see that now. Don't you?'

His heart forgot to beat. His lungs forgot to inhale. He'd held on to his bitterness—his need to get even—for nine years.

His veins pulsed and twitched in his cheek. 'It seems I do.'

He was so *angry*.

Angry with her, angry with her dad, angry with himself and with the past he had no control over. Damien Hegarty had manipulated him into believing Charlotte didn't want him, and her dad had convinced her that he hadn't shown up. They'd both been tricked—catapulted away from their destinies.

And you have no control over your present either, do you? Your father made sure of that.

He pushed the voice down, because he *could* control *this*. He ached. Throbbed with the need to lose himself in anything but the past and how wrong he'd been. How naïve he'd allowed himself to be. How fragile he'd allowed her rejection to make him. He'd lumped her rejection in with all the others he'd experienced since he was a child.

Since the rejection of his father.

Yes, his father had claimed him eventually—but only because he was the only one available. *He'd wanted him for his blood.* Not for himself alone. He'd knocked that boy out of him. Moulded him into what he'd wanted.

But Charlotte...

He'd been wrong.

Her hand moved, her fingertips rising to his cheek. 'Akeem...'

His name sounded as if it had been torn from her lips. A breathless question. *A plea?*

They were both reeling from the revelation of her father's trickery. She was asking him to give her somewhere to hide—someone to hide in. Wasn't she? And just for a moment he would let her hide in him. In the intensity crackling between them as hot and wild as it had when he was between her thighs.

For one last time he would surrender to it. To the pull. *To her.*

Unable to contain the emotions building in his chest, he crushed her mouth against his. He let all his rage pour into her as he moved his lips against hers. And she kissed him back, her lips smacking against his, fanning the flames licking between them.

He couldn't stand it. The agony. He tore his mouth from hers, his breathing ragged. He couldn't do anything but focus on his next intake of air.

Pushing her away from him, he panted as hard as she did.

His need for revenge was unwarranted.

His insides clenched. All along he should have been giving his attention to his duty.

He should apologise. He closed his eyes. He couldn't. What would he be apologising for? For everything he was—*had been*—and for what everyone kept telling him wasn't enough? For believing she'd thought the same?

Akeem opened his eyes.

He grabbed her hand and pulled her inside his elevator in the sky.

'This elevator,' he said, releasing her hand and turning to face her. 'Is revolutionary in the aircraft industry. One of the first of its kind. My father was many things, but he always liked to be among the first. The first to win, the first to lose. But most of all he put himself first. Before his wife, his mistresses, his son and his kingdom.'

He turned away from her and pressed a button. Then he turned to face the doors, watching them close and seal him inside the elevator with the woman beside him, her reflection mirrored in the reflective doors.

His future Queen.

'I am not my father. I will marry because my duty to my country will demand it. But I will not succumb to the madness of passion again. My people will always come first,' he said.

Because he needed the reminder of who he was now, and so did she.

'You will always come second after we leave this plane.'

CHAPTER FIVE

'WHY WOULD YOU say something like that?' Her voice was small, and she hated it. Hated it that he'd made her feel that way.

Invisible.

'It's a simple truth you should understand,' he replied.

She snapped her gaze to the impenetrable figure beside her. *Understand what?* All her life she'd been under no illusion. She came second. Or last, if at all. And now, after everything that had been revealed—*her dad!*—he was asking her to put up, shut up, and do as she was told. Step aside for someone else. Forget her feelings—her needs because he said so. Like her dad.

She didn't think so.

Her dad had betrayed her. She bit hard at the inside of her cheek, stemming the tears, the anger burning in her chest. She had been his daughter. His *daughter*! And he'd lied. Tricked her. Manipulated her into staying in his shadow. Into helping him live his life while she forgot about hers.

She was tired of forgetting.

She wanted to live her way, and for herself first.

Her shoulders tight, her breathing rapid, she didn't allow herself to think the thought through. She stepped in front of Akeem, raised her hand, and smacked her palm against the big red button.

The lift shuddered to a standstill.

'What are you doing?' he asked.

'You don't get to talk to me like that,' she said, wishing her heart would beat normally, not with this frantic, chaotic drumroll it had had since he'd waltzed back into her life. She shrugged it off, made herself meet those eyes, fixed on her with disapproval. 'You don't get to speak to me like I don't matter—or *won't* matter,' she corrected, and pointed to the closed doors, 'after we step outside.'

'How would you like me to speak to you?'

The question was flat, with no hint of sarcasm or genuine curiosity. Only words.

She'd seen so many versions of Akeem today: the man with furious kisses whose hurt had been as visceral as her own when they'd confronted the past. *When they'd kissed.* And then there was the man who would be King. The man who'd faced their unannounced visitors without so much as a blush, and come back to demand she be his bride.

The Akeem she was looking at now was already King. No explosion of passion, just a cool regard. The King was looking at her now, and he didn't see her. Not the way he had when he'd stripped her to her skin and pushed her into demanding what she wanted.

No, this was a king who saw nothing but his people.

His duty.

'You asked me to be your Queen and help you establish yourself as King in the eyes of your people—'

'And for me to do that they must come before you.'

'No.'

'It is not negotiable,' he dismissed.

'A lot has happened since London.' She blew out an exasperated breath. 'A lot neither of us expected. But you're not the only one who gets to set the rules.'

'It is my job to set the rules, and to have them obeyed without question.'

'Not with me. Not any more. Not after—'

'Your father?'

His interjection was low. Quiet. But just as he had in the limo and before he'd ordered her to rest, or when he'd stripped her bare in the lounge, he knew exactly what she meant—what she needed—before she'd voiced it.

He did still see her—even if the crown of duty was obscuring his sight.

She could feel it.

The *knowing* between them.

She nodded slowly. 'My dad manipulated me,

and I sacrificed the last nine years of my life to care for him because he tricked me into it.'

Her head hurt. Her heart hurt. Her father and her grief were complicated, but she still missed him. *Loved him.* But…

'Don't pretend there are choices when there aren't any choices to be made,' she said. 'There is only what *you* want. Just like my dad.'

'I am nothing like your father.'

'Maybe you don't *want* to be like him—'

'I am *nothing* like him,' he repeated, his voice a sharp warning. 'Or my own father.'

'Did you love him?'

The pause was pregnant.

'Your dad?' she clarified. 'I loved mine, but I'm not sure he loved me, because he forgot about his duty to me—'

'Stop comparing our lives. They are not similar,' he bit, and the hard edge to his voice hurt.

'But they *are* similar,' she contradicted. 'You can't deny that.'

'Maybe once,' he conceded. 'Once we walked the same streets in the same shoes. But not any more. That world is no longer mine, and it never will be again.'

'I was an accident—like you,' she continued, ignoring his resistance. 'Mum and Dad got married because of me, and continued their binge drinking regardless of the fact they'd made a life. My mum died because of her continued carelessness, and I paid the price by becoming a full-time carer for my dad.'

Their eyes met again in the mirror.

'Dad forgot that he should take care of me, and not the other way around. He forgot his duty so badly he tricked me into staying in that role for another nine years...'

She trailed off as flashes of the last nine years hit her. She'd lost so much time. How many people had she lost? How many friendships? Her career as an artist?

'You paid the price because your dad couldn't keep it in his pants and you ended up in care. I ended up in care too.' She watched as he hardened at the reminder of how they'd met. Both lost. Alone. Needing what the other had to give.

Sanctuary.

'I know you were there much longer than I was. I got to go home when you didn't have a home to go to. But...' She shrugged. 'Forgetting about myself—putting myself last—isn't something I can agree to again.'

'I will not forget my people as my father did and allow *your* hurt feelings—'

'As King, your duty comes first.' She inhaled deeply, steeling herself to ask for what she wanted. *Needed.* 'But I need you to be a decent human being. No throwaway comments. Explain what you mean and why you want something. Don't hurt my feelings to get what you want.'

He grimaced. 'Feelings cannot win. We cannot put them first,' he continued. 'Because when you do, you end up in situations you never would otherwise.'

'Like losing nine years of your life because of your lying, treacherous father?' she asked. 'Like being promised a night of sex only to be trapped into getting married? Like agreeing to be your ex-lover's wife, only to be told you won't matter in the marriage, anyway?'

Her rant over, she glared at him. At the skin tightly pulled across his cheeks. At his flaring nostrils. At his eyes, dark and wide.

'Feelings don't always have to be so...*extreme*,' she started again when he didn't answer.

'We have been nothing *but* extreme, Charlotte,' he corrected. His voice was a low rumble. 'How can we be anything else?'

'So you've decided for both of us that it's all or nothing? No middle ground? No compromise?'

'Kings do not compromise.'

'What about friends?' She swallowed hard. 'What about husbands?'

'Friends?' He flinched, and she swallowed down the pain in her throat.

Akeem held her gaze as something unidentifiable flashed in his eyes, with the silence hanging between them.

'I cannot promise you friendship. I cannot promise you everything you have asked for.'

She opened her mouth to speak, but he shook his head.

'I'm not finished.'

She pressed her lips together, and he continued.

'But I can promise to treat you as a human being, and to respect that you are a woman who can make her own decisions. Going forward, I will ask,' he promised, moving in on her, 'not demand.'

His voice was silk against her frayed edges. His words. His promise. This might not be the life she wanted, but she could shape it into something good if he would *see* her. Recognise that she would not remain in the background any more.

She would voice her opinions.

She would matter.

She pressed the red button again and the lift rattled, picked up a little speed, and stopped with an ungraceful thump.

He hit a button and the doors opened. A red carpet ran all the way from under the plane to a convoy of cars and a gathering of men.

And a helicopter.

'You are shoeless,' he said, and she looked at him, then looked at her feet. 'May I carry you?' he asked, his words articulated with effort.

She smiled at the tightness of his mouth. 'I can walk,' she assured him.

Because she could. She could walk forward with her head high and her feet bare because she wanted to. Because it was *her* choice.

Before he could comment again, she moved in front of him and onto the red carpet, through the parting throng of men and towards the helicopter doors, magically opened by invisible staff.

She climbed inside and Akeem was quickly beside her, pulling a harness over her shoulders, between her breasts, and clipping her in between her thighs with quick and steady hands, before climbing in beside her in the pilot's seat.

Her stomach lurched. '*You're* flying it?'

He turned to her. 'Scared?'

'No,' she denied. But the truth was she was exhausted with being afraid, and this moment, these changes of events, her agreeing to be Queen—

What if the people didn't accept her as their Queen? Her dad had never loved her. If he couldn't love her, his own daughter, how could anyone else? How could a whole desert kingdom accept her when her family hadn't?

But how would she know if she didn't try?

She'd been afraid most of her life.

Afraid of never being accepted.

Afraid to fail…

The rotor blades turned. The sound was getting louder and louder, replicating the whooshing inside her ears.

She gasped as the helicopter turned in a three-sixty and took flight. All around her was desert. Miles of it. Before the city sprang up from the red sands themselves.

It was something both ancient and surreal. A wall spanned the city at the base of the mountain, and buildings with rounded peaks stood on tall columns and archways. And up it rose. The city ascended into the skies. And there, in the distance, above the walled city, was a palace set against the mountains.

'It's a fortress!' she exclaimed.

A calming realisation washed over her. The doubts and the fears were her dad's, because her sixteen-year-old self was still inside her. She could feel her, kicking inside her chest and demanding Charlotte take this second chance being offered to her.

On her terms she would claim back her art and her identity. Because this was her ticket to adventure.

To life…

She wouldn't fail this time.

Failure was *not* built into her DNA.

She flicked a glance at Akeem. Confident. At ease. Intuitively, she felt safe—protected. But wasn't that the most dangerous illusion of all? Because the scariest of all the things that were changing around her was *him*, and the part of herself that saw this as a second chance with Akeem.

Turning away from him, she refused to acknowledge *that* part, and focused on the views before her. On the golden globe of the sun descending behind the mountains and turning the

sky a deep orange and the landscape beneath—
a mystical brilliance of burning red, golden
spires piercing the skies from doomed roofs, and
splashes of green feathered throughout.

Taliedaa was breathtaking.

She watched, entranced, as with complete, confident control Akeem flew them towards the palace in the sky.

To her new home.

Where adventure waited.

He'd hungered for this. For nine years he'd
dreamt of this moment—ached for it. Ached to
rub all she'd thrown away to live a life of drudgery in her face. To shame her for doubting him.
To hold the past by the hand and show it there was
no place in his world for it now.

To show it—*her*—all he had become.

But her betrayal had never existed.

And now she would have a place in his world.

He unbuckled his harness and exited the chop-
per. Motioning to the staff at the gilded entrance to
wait, he moved to Charlotte's door and wrenched
it open.

He looked down at her feet. Her bare feet were
slender and long, with a high instep. Elegant. *Un-
adorned.* Ready to be embellished. He would have
her toes painted. His eyes moved over the green
robes covering her body. He could wrap her in

silk, but could she become the Queen he needed her to be? Could she leave the past on the plane?

He met her eyes.

Could he?

Palms forward, she said, 'Don't carry me.'

'Do you have a hidden pair of slippers?'

'No.'

'There is no carpet to cushion your feet here,' he said.

'Are you asking me if I can or telling me I can't walk?'

He bit the inside of his cheek. 'I am asking.'

'Then ask.'

He reached for her but she halted him.

'Questions require words,' she said, 'and I would like to hear yours. I'd like to hear your respect for the woman I am...a woman who can make her own decisions.'

His eyes flicked to the staff waiting for his command to come and greet them. He should cloak himself in his armour and become the Crown Prince—rightful heir to the Taliedaaen throne. He had been him for so long—the son of a king—it should feel like a second skin. *But it didn't.* He felt crumpled. Dishevelled. As if someone beneath his suit of armour was stretching the seams...

'May I?' he asked tightly, and she nodded.

He reached for her again. This time, she didn't resist. She came to him with open palms on his shoulders. He drew her in tight against him, feeling the quick inhale-exhale of her breath, and with one hand beneath her thigh, one around her waist, he carried her, step by step, to the front door of the royal palace.

Pride.

It burned in his belly.

'Your Royal Highness… Miss Hegarty…' the staff chorused.

Never had he thought to hear his title along with her name. He kept walking because his hands refused to release her, his feet refused to stop.

Formal introductions could wait.

What he needed couldn't.

Distance.

Akeem stepped into the tiled entrance hall with its high domed roof and kept walking. He turned into a hallway lavishly decorated with ancient tiles depicting scenes of palace life, then walked through a courtyard lit with lanterns powered by unseen electricity and opened a door.

He hadn't held his past by the hand, he recognised. He'd carried it through the front door and welcomed it. Claimed it as his and given it a home. He'd turned his past into a spectacle of duty, and now he was bound.

Tethered.

He slid her to her feet, caught her wrist, and pulled her into the room with him, onto a floor littered with silk rugs. He closed the door. Her wrist was too small, too delicate. He dropped it.

She didn't move. She stayed too close…too near.

'Charlotte, you are not blinking.'

She blinked unnaturally several times. 'I'm not?'

'No.'

'I'm sorry. I'm a little overawed,' she admitted. 'The helicopter, the desert, the city… The *palace*,' she crooned. 'It's beautiful, Akeem. Your home is beautiful…'

His pulse was refusing to slow and his chest puffed. Her mouth was saying all the right words, but they didn't stroke his ego the way he'd thought they would. The *but* lingering on her tongue was too loud, too sharp—not what he had envisaged.

Nothing so far was what he'd envisaged his time with Charlotte would be.

And whose fault is that?

'But…?' he encouraged, keeping his voice even and ignoring the thud of his temples.

'But…' she started, and flicked her tongue against the dip in her bottom lip. 'But this is my adventure. I want to know what happens next before it happens—before you hoist me over your shoulder again.'

'Adventure?' he repeated, his brain refusing to understand her use of that word in correlation with his life. 'This is not—'

'An unusual, exciting or daring experience. That is the definition of adventure, and I'm pretty sure this fits the bill.'

'You have a dictionary with you?'

'I like words. I've read the dictionary quite a few times. Just for fun.' She slanted a slender shoulder. 'So adventurous was my life before you.'

'Then tell me what you make of this word.' He moved towards her. Closer. And whispered, 'Box…'

'Box?' she repeated, lips pursed.

'You want to know what happens next on this adventure of yours?' he asked. She nodded. 'Then tell me: what is the definition of box?'

'It depends—'

'No,' he said, redirecting her. 'A box—an everyday box. What is it?'

'A container with a lid.'

'Exactly. But sometimes boxes have locks. This box will need a lock.'

She pushed the scarf from her hair and let it hang on her shoulders. 'Is this a lesson?'

'Perhaps,' he said, resisting the urge to close the distance between them and push his hands into her hair, clench his fists around the curling softness. 'You will need a box.'

'A box?'

'A large box,' he agreed, and then he closed the distance between them and did what he'd told himself he wouldn't. He touched her. A finger to her cheek. So warm. So soft. 'Staff will enter this room when I leave, and they will help you pack it.'

'Pack it?' she asked.

He moved his finger. Slowly. Down her cheek. He stopped at her chin and tilted it. Made her look at him as he moved his finger over the notch beneath her throat, down between her breasts and flattened his palm on her ribcage.

On her heart.

'How many years has your heart been beating?'

'That's a strange question.'

The words shuddered from her lips and he felt it. Her hiccup. The double beat of her heart beneath his palm. She was faltering.

'And that is not an answer.'

'Depends on who you ask.'

'How old are you?'

'You know how old I am.'

'Indulge me.'

'Twenty-five.'

'For twenty-five years you have felt every feeling, every doubt, every fear, and now you will let them go.' His palm pushed into her and massaged the flesh, caging her heart.

'Let them go…?' she breathed.

'You will not entertain them again,' he said, and then corrected himself with a speed that surprised him. 'Unless you want to. Keep the key if you must—if you *like*,' he said. 'But a queen must know control. Which emotion to display. Which fear to make use of to drive her. And you will be Queen, Charlotte. You will understand control.'

A sound escaped her lips and fired straight into

his groin. Half-moan, half-sigh. He wanted to taste it. Inhale it—feed his lungs, his life's essence. But he resisted, and he would keep on resisting.

'Pack your feelings away,' he encouraged, and then he told her what he'd told himself on his first night here. 'Put them in a box, *qalbi*, and forget them.'

'Is that what you do, Akeem?'

She waved a hand towards the bed and he turned to it. It was across the room. White organza drapes fell from wooden posts, and on it was a mattress so deep…

'Are all your feelings hiding under that bed?'

He snapped his attention back to her. 'I do not need a box,' he lied. 'All I need is here.' He touched his chest. 'An armour called duty.'

'Tell me.'

She pressed her hand to his chest.

Oh, but his heart hammered.

Thud, thud, thud.

'What was it like for you?' she asked.

And he did not like it. Her ability to call to the part of him he'd buried deep. So deep. He no longer had the key to his box. If it had ever had a key—a lock. But the lid was creaking back from its rusted hinges, and it hurt.

'What was it like?' he repeated, all too conscious of his hand on her body, of hers on his. 'I learnt how to represent my people. Not with wealth or pomp, but by using the privilege of being Crown Prince to guide a people. A country.'

'Who taught you how to do that? To understand?'

'Them. The people,' he said. 'They were talking, but my father wasn't listening. I listened.'

He had been right to become Akeem Abd al-Uzza and banish the boy Charlotte had known. The boy who had freely felt his feelings. Because now, moving forward, he wouldn't let himself feel anything for her.

It was the way he'd survived for nine years, and the only way he would survive now.

His father had abused his power to satisfy himself at the cost of so many people's lives. His people would not suffer the same under his rule. Not because of his negligence. His *feelings*.

'It can't have been easy for you—'

He stepped back, pulled his hand away as hers fell from his chest. He did not want her to see—to know—how hard it had been for him. He wanted her to know only that he was *this*. A man of royalty. A would-be king. A crown prince. Anything but a basic boy with basic needs...

'I have never known anything easy.'

'Will it be hard for me?' she asked.

'The quicker you understand that everything you do from this moment will be to take care of something bigger than you or me, the easier the next steps will be for you,' he said.

'Like looking after my dad? That was bigger than me—than my dreams.'

He tilted his head to look at her. 'I know you understand sacrifice—'

'And this will be another?'

'No, not completely,' he denied. Because that part was true. He would pay for her time. Her sacrifices. 'This time you will keep your art. Whatever you need—ask. Selma will be with you shortly.'

'Selma?'

'Your personal assistant.'

'How long do I have to pack?' She laughed when he stared at her. 'My box?'

'Three days,' he answered.

Because he needed those three days away from her. Three days to compose himself. To stamp out whatever was between them. To put it back into his dreams, where only the darkness recognised its poignancy.

'What happens then?'

'We shall present our engagement to the people of Taliedaa. To dignitaries, the Royal Council…' He inhaled deeply. 'The world and its cameras will stand in the gardens of the palace as we stand above them on the royal balcony, and *nothing*,' he emphasised, 'nothing other than control and orchestrated smiles should be with us. Everything else—'

'Should be in the box?'

'Well done.'

She shook her head. 'I have less than three days to reinvent myself?'

'Not reinvent,' he clarified. 'Refine. My staff will help you,' he said, and then corrected himself. '*Your* staff will help you prepare for the announcement of our engagement and for our wedding.'

'Wedding?'

'One week from today.'

'A week?' she gasped. 'Why so fast?'

'We must be married before I take the crown,' he explained. 'That is why every decision—every item you pack away—is crucial.'

She nodded. Small continuous nods. 'Will I see you before?'

'No.' He turned away from her, ignoring the pull to stay with her—to stay *close*—and opened the door.

'That's it? That's all you're going to say?'

He didn't look back. 'There is nothing else to say, Charlotte,' he told her over his shoulder. 'Find a way to forget the woman you are and become a queen.'

Just like he had.

He closed the door without a second glance and walked back the way he'd came.

He had three days to bury his box deeper. Because he would not reveal what was inside.

Or who...

CHAPTER SIX

HE'D DISMISSED HER. Left her to prepare on her own for a situation she'd never dreamt she'd be in. Three days to turn herself into a queen. One week until she became a wife.

She wasn't ready. How could she be? She was Charlotte Hegarty, survivor of addict parents. The daughter of alcoholics. What right did she have to these things now being offered to her?

She closed her eyes.

She would not fail.

Her dad had been wrong.

'*Shukran.*'

'*Hasan jidana.*'

Selma, her personal assistant, smiled. 'Very good, Your Royal Highness.'

Charlotte wriggled in a little celebration dance and pressed her toes into the bedspread.

'Charlotte,' she corrected for the umpteenth time. She wasn't royal yet. She was a royal-in-waiting until tomorrow, and even then... *Your Royal Highness?*

'You cannot learn a language with many nuances in a few days,' said Selma.

Charlotte crossed her legs. 'I know.'

'In time, you will learn,' Selma soothed her impatient student. 'The palace will provide a tutor—'

'A tutor can't teach me what you can before the announcement.'

'Of course it is your choice, but the brain is much like a sandwich.' Selma pressed her palms together as she sat on the edge of the bed 'Too many ingredients and the filling spills out.' She clapped. *'Splodge.'*

Charlotte laughed. Hard. And then covered her mouth with her hand.

'It won't be funny when you can't remember anything because you've tried to digest too much and your stomach is still full and yet you must eat more sandwiches.'

'Are you hungry, Selma?' she asked, displacing her hand from her mouth. 'All your analogies are about food. You should have eaten with me. There was way too much food for just one person!'

'I'm always hungry—and you are always hungry for knowledge, yes?' Brown eyes twinkled beneath dark arched brows. 'Because you eat very little and ask many questions?'

'Nerves,' she confessed easily. 'It seems important to know as much as I can about my new home, and you've been an excellent teacher.'

'The best way to gain new knowledge is to let it sit with you.' She pointed to the mountain of plump pillows at Charlotte's back. 'Sleep, and let your subconscious do the hard work.'

'I don't think I'll sleep.'

She hadn't slept well since she'd arrived, and the thought of tomorrow's schedule wound her up too tightly to sleep now. Her eyes wandered longingly to the box of supplies she'd been gifted, which was sitting beside the low-slung sofa on the far side of the room. Her fingers itched to pull the paper free, to take the pencils from the packs and escape into herself.

Art. It was right there. Waiting for her to claim it. As it had been every night since her arrival. The one thing that made her *her*. She pushed down the longing because only later, when she was alone, would she continue to rediscover that part of herself.

'But you must rest.' She pulled her gaze back to Selma. 'Go.' She shooed her off the bed with the back of her hand. 'I'm so sorry… I didn't think…' She paused.

Selma had offered her something achingly close to friendship. She knew the dynamics were all wrong, but somehow it worked. *A friend.* Maybe soon a confidante? Her heart bloomed. She'd had no one to share her secrets with. No one since

Akeem. But the moment Selma had introduced herself they'd hit it off.

'It's been so nice,' Charlotte continued. 'Thank you for making it nice, Selma.'

These last three days she hadn't been alone. Her days had been full, but her nights…

Akeem hadn't returned.

'You won't thank me tomorrow, after the stylist has plucked you within an inch of your life—'

'Like a chicken?'

Selma wrinkled her nose. 'And told a gazillion facts you'll never remember about Taliedaa by Kadar. He never knows where to begin or where to end. But he is passionate about his records, and continues to preserve the legacy of our young sovereign state. He's overjoyed that you are such an eager student, but tomorrow I will rein him in.'

'No, please don't.'

'There is too much to do for his lesson to go over its allotted time.'

'It's been fascinating, meeting with him every day over breakfast—he obviously loves this place.'

'He does.' Selma flushed. 'Very much.'

'And you?'

'I love him—but don't tell him.' She smiled, but the corners of her lips pointed down. 'He wouldn't know where to store *that* insignificant fact in his history books.'

'Maybe it doesn't have to be history?' Charlotte said—because hadn't her past very much become her present? If she could have a second chance, couldn't anyone?

Is that how you see this? As a second chance with Akeem?

Selma was shaking her head, and Charlotte ignored the punch of the question she'd asked herself.

She concentrated on the woman on her bed. 'Have you and Kadar known each other long?'

Selma coughed and rose, clearly not wanting to talk about Kadar further. 'Would you like me to help you settle down?'

'No, I'll manage.'

No one had ever offered to tuck her in before. Selma offered every night. Maybe she could ask her to check under the bed... Her stomach pulled. She didn't have to ask. She knew what would be under there. *Her fears.* But she wouldn't be afraid. She would let them go, as Akeem had told her.

'Sleep?' Selma suggested. 'Tomorrow will be—'

'Scary?'

'Busy,' she corrected. 'Your history lesson with breakfast, and now the designers have your preferences and sizes...' She smiled brightly, her warm brown eyes widening. 'You will have more than the off-the-rack collection they've left you to get by with.'

'All these clothes...' Charlotte smoothed her hand over the layered silk organza dress she'd chosen to wear for tomorrow's lessons beside her on the bed. 'They aren't off the rack where I shop.'

'Where do you shop in England? London—so many shops!'

She picked up the dress and held it against her chest. 'Charity shops mainly,' Charlotte confessed, refusing to feel any shame. She loved charity shops. They'd kept her clothed throughout her teens and into adulthood, and her dad too. But she'd never have found clothes like *these* there.

She looked down at the brown dress. *No.* What had they called it? *Plum chestnut?* It was layered and striped. *It was beautiful.* It was a V-necked asymmetric style, with batwing sleeves, a fitted waist and a flared skirt, and a lop-sided hem overlaid by sheer panels...

She never had anything so exquisite next to her skin. And she loved it.

Was that materialistic? Probably. She didn't care. Wasn't it every girl's fantasy to have her Cinderella moment? Her whole life she'd known how she'd wanted to look, but she'd just never been able to afford it.

Akeem as a fairy godmother? She smothered the cackle in her throat.

The team who'd joined her very quickly after Akeem's departure from her room had supplied her with underwear, shoes, daywear, nightwear... In every colour she could think of and some she wouldn't have considered. *Umber?* She'd never worn umber...or burnt orange...or red...

Her core tightened. Tomorrow she would. Tomorrow she'd wear red.

'Well, no charity shop bags will enter the palace tomorrow morning.'

Selma winked, and held out her hand for the dress. Charlotte loved her familiarity. Her ease as she took the dress from her and hung it, ready for tomorrow.

'The designers will return with a wardrobe.' Selma whistled, long and low. 'A wardrobe with you in mind on so many rails.' Selma clapped. 'I can't wait to see their designs for your wedding dress.'

Charlotte's stomach dipped. She couldn't think about the wedding yet. She wasn't officially engaged, and her fiancé had gone missing...

She missed him, she acknowledged, but only to herself.

'And, of course, your finished engagement outfit...' Selma sighed wistfully, a hand on her chest. *'That dress.'*

Nerves made Charlotte's fingers bite into her palm. 'One dress at a time, Selma,' she chided playfully. Because that was exactly what she was doing. Taking one dress—one day at a time.

'Both will be perfect.'

She didn't doubt it.

But what about the woman *in* the dress?

For seventy-two hours she'd been in his home. Under his roof. And he'd resisted her. He'd controlled his impulse to seek her out, to replay their encounter in the flesh, to touch her—hold her...

Hold her?

Akeem toyed with the black leather strap in his hand, frayed and cracked from age. He'd always been impulsive as a child—and as a teenager. He'd said what he was thinking—*reacted.* He was no longer impulsive. Leaving her alone in his palace, depositing her in her rooms and stepping away—they were considered choices.

He'd given himself space—taken active steps towards addressing the intensity of his feelings for Charlotte. They were too intense. Everything he could not allow himself to feel.

No, you've just hidden from her like a scared little boy.

He was not little, and he was not afraid. He'd been working with his most senior aides from dawn till dusk to make this day move like a well-oiled machine. Everything was in place. Everything was ready.

All he had to do was wait twelve more hours...

He ran his fingers over the edges of the watch until he came to its small, round metal face. The silver-plated back was tarnished, with a copperish rim showing its worth.

Cheap.

You shouldn't have that, should you? Put it back under the bed like a good boy.

He wasn't *that* little boy any more.

If your father knew you had it—

He was dead. He couldn't do anything any more.

But Akeem knew exactly what his father would have done. He would have had one of his men take it. He would have laid it on the table in front of his throne and then he would have called him. Made him watch as he brought a heavy hammer down onto the glass face. Smashed it. The basic wristwatch of a basic woman. Just to smother the basic love of a boy for his basic mother.

So why do you still have it, Would-Be King? Do you need it? Will you cry without it?

His hand squeezed around the watch in his hand until it dug deeply into his palm.

Pain. He flexed his fingers. He welcomed it.

You didn't welcome it nine years ago, when you confronted your father on his pretty throne.

He shoved the watch into his pocket, but the intrusive thought persisted. He spat a curse to the rising sun, and the memory of the last time he'd seen the dawn with Charlotte emerged as vividly as if he were watching a replay.

The morning after they'd both lost their virginity.

The morning he'd said things would be different.

The morning he'd promised they'd make their own family—*be* a family.

Turning his back on the city, Akeem moved through the rooms he called his and, with the past biting at his heels, walked towards Charlotte's rooms.

Outside her room, he hesitated. Could he really not resist for twelve more hours? Had the last seventy-two hours been for nothing…?

He swept inside without knocking.

The balcony doors were open, and there she stood outside. Her body was covered in an organza dress and her hair hung between her shoulder blades in a loose ponytail.

Moving towards her, across the hardwood floor littered with silk rugs and past the vast bed, he detested the blood heating through him at the sight of her. Detested this tug inside him. It was the sensation of a rope being pulled so tightly that he couldn't withstand it for twelve more hours.

Before he could stop himself, he called out to her. 'Charlotte.'

She didn't turn.

He stopped statue-still, a foot before the balcony doors, and half turned, ready to leave as he'd entered. Unobserved. But she turned first.

'Akeem?'

He inched closer, calling for the control he needed. 'Are you drawing?' he asked.

'Only sketching…' She looked down at the pad resting on the stone balustrade and brushed a hand over it. 'It's not very good.'

Memories, fast and blinding, hurtled towards him and plunged him into the past… Under the oak tree. *Laughing*. Handing her a sketchpad and newly acquired pencils, bought with his meagre wages. Her eyes moving over him as he'd sat and sat and she'd drawn him.

'How does it feel?' he asked. 'To draw again?'

A shy smile curved her lips. 'Like wearing my favourite pyjamas when they've just come out the tumble dryer. Comfortable,' she explained with a half-laugh, half-sigh. 'Worn in.'

'Bring it to me,' he demanded, wanting to see— *needing* to see.

'No, it isn't ready.' She turned her sketchpad over and turned all her attention to him.

'You would deny the Crown Prince?' he asked.

'No, I would deny *you*, Akeem. It's not ready.'

'Come to me,' he commanded.

Tentatively, she took a step towards him. Another step. The shawl fell from her shoulders to the stone floor. He'd approved her dress, as he'd approved the rest of her temporary wardrobe, but seeing it on her in the flesh, her tawny beige skin alight with golden undertones... His throat dried and his groin pulsed.

He reached into his pocket and pulled out the small watch. He enclosed his thumb and forefinger around her wrist and fastened it there with quick fingers. Not letting himself notice the delicate flesh of the inner side of her wrist, or how delicate and how soft the skin felt as his fingers brushed against it. Neither did he let himself analyse why he was doing this. Only accepted that he was.

'It's a watch...'

'It was my mother's.'

Charlotte placed her hand on his. He looked at their hands, hers so much smaller. She trusted him. Trusted him to cage the fire within him. The passion. Just as his mother had trusted his father to do the right thing when he'd seduced her away from her duties and made her take a leap of faith into his arms.

And then he'd crushed her.

Her reputation.

Her heart.

He snatched his hand away.

He did not want Charlotte's heart.

She rubbed her wrist. 'Why would you give me your mother's watch?'

He stepped back. He was eighteen again, confused, giving Charlotte his extra pillow.

No. He was twenty-seven and a crown prince. He was not confused.

'I don't need it any more,' he told her—because he didn't. He didn't want to feel attached to the past. To the boy that no one wanted, lost in the care system.

'You don't need it?' she croaked. 'It was your mum's?'

'I can't give you everything you asked for on the plane. So I am giving you this.'

'What can't you give me?'

'Decency.'

'You can't be *decent*?' She laughed. 'Why not?'

'Because I do not feel decent when I'm around you.'

Her smile vanished. 'Is that why you haven't come to me?' she asked. 'Why you've stayed away?'

He didn't answer. He couldn't. How could he admit he'd stayed away because every time he was with her it was a fight? A constant battle with his control?

'You've stayed away because you're angry, haven't you?'

Nine years and his smiles were practised...*perfect*. He did not show his feelings, let alone speak them out loud. But she could see.

He clamped his teeth together.

She stepped into his space and it hit him like a stray bullet. The presence of her. The calming balm she'd offered to him so many years ago, when he'd been about to leave the care system and embark on his own journey. A journey with her. And here they were again. *Embarking.*

She raised her hand and he made himself remain still. Quiet. All but for the thumping in his chest as she placed her palm to his cheek.

'You're angry with the past. With me. I get it. But I'm not angry. Not with you for staying away. Or with my dad.' She smiled. That small knowing smile. 'Because the past is the reason I'm here, in this beautiful dress, watching the sun rise over red hills and a city made of red stone. Am I still afraid of getting it wrong?'

Her eyes, emeralds embedded in gold, blazed and she caught him inside the flames.

'Of course I am. I've been getting things wrong my whole life. And my dad was in my head too long for him to disappear with an outrageous marriage proposal. But I'm here.'

Her hand moved down his cheek to his shoulder. A slide of her palm and every nerve-ending came alive under her touch.

He resisted. Stood still. Resolute.

She placed her palm over his heart. 'And so are you.'

'And so am I…' His reply was raw. Rough. He wasn't supposed to be here. He should be in his own rooms. He should be anywhere but here, letting her touch him. *Soothe him.*

'You told me feelings shouldn't matter here, but can you feel it?'

He could feel everything.

'Feel what?' he asked, denying that her touch did anything but pull at his groin.

'The past paving the way to the future.'

'Maybe for you. But for me…'

'You are to be the next King.'

He didn't answer. His every action since he'd stepped into this room had not been *kingly.*

She tilted her head. 'What makes you so afraid of your feelings? Of mine?'

'I am not afraid.'

'I am—but not of my feelings. Whatever has brought you here this morning, and whatever has kept you away since we got here, it isn't because you don't feel. It's because you *do*. I see you confronting the past—our shared past—' she watched him with compressed lips '—and it hurts.'

'I am not in pain,' he dismissed angrily. 'I do not feel pain.'

'Of course you do,' she contradicted him, her eyes zeroing in on his face, moving across every taut vein, the thrust of his hard jaw. 'If you weren't in pain, you wouldn't look at me like I'm an alien because I'm calm about a betrayal that affected us both.'

His eyes stayed on her plush little mouth, that was saying, oh, so sweetly, all the words he didn't want to hear. *Shared betrayal. Shared rejection. A shared past!* He did not want to hear them, let alone speak of them.

He could silence those lips—pin her tongue against his and stop it wagging.

She stepped back. *One step. Two steps. Three.* It would take him less than a millisecond to correct her error. It was a mistake to make him chase her. Hunt her.

She tilted her chin at him, elongating her throat. She was luring him away from duty, trapping him inside himself, and he wanted the heat of her on him. Not these feelings causing his chest to tighten and his temples to throb. He wanted *her* to throb. He wanted—

'Tell me why you're here,' she said.

Wisps of hair had escaped her ponytail and

were curling haphazardly under her ears. He wanted to release the trapped mass, let it fall about her shoulders. Feel its thickness in his hands.

He stilled. 'I never should have come.'

'Akeem—'

'Shush.' He silenced her attempt to speak, but really he was turning up the volume on the song of duty that he could never mute. It was always playing, and whatever the volume he could hear it—because it came from within…because it lived inside him.

He would not allow this energy between them to leave these rooms. He had a duty to deny his needs—even the basic needs of a man—and show the people of Taliedaa he would not abandon them for pleasure. He would not abandon them as his father had. As his father had abandoned his mother. *Him.*

Charlotte had known the boy. Akeem Ali. The son of Yamina Ali.

He took a breath, filled his lungs, and made himself stand straight. Tall. *Privileged.*

She did not know this man.

She did not know the King.

Charlotte felt it. The shift.

It wasn't a dramatic change. It was a change in the atmosphere. Akeem's head was bare, his hair ruffled, his bearded jaw squared, and his black tunic hung loosely from his broad shoulders. But inside his muscles were taut. Her eyes moved down his throat to the V-neck collar. He reflected nothing but steel, even though his clothing was relaxed.

'You never should have come at all,' she said. 'If you didn't—'

'Didn't what?'

'Didn't want me. I know you wanted the girl you thought I was. A one-night stand. But this woman in front of you now. She is an unwanted queen—'

'Wanting is not the problem. *This*—' he waved his hands between them '—is the problem.'

'Me?'

'This intensity.'

'You came to me,' she reminded him. 'Not the other way around.'

'I came because I understand—*intimately*—the disorientation of having nothing to ground you to a world that has been thrust upon you. I wanted you to have something—'

'Something to ground me?'

'Yes,' he lied. Because he'd come here because he hadn't been able to fight it. The need to be close. *The pull.* But he would fight it now. He would fight it with everything he was.

'And when you came in here the past caught up with you?'

'Not the past, Charlotte,' he said. *'You.'*

'At St John's I came to find you, didn't I?' she said.

She'd sneaked past the resident care workers and sought him out. She'd found him asleep and she hadn't had to say anything. Together they'd crept into the gardens, hand in hand, and hidden under that oak tree.

She'd told him everything. And when she had voiced all the secrets she'd been told to keep quiet—never to tell outsiders—he'd simply held her. He'd let her feel all the feelings she'd kept at bay her entire life.

'It is not the same,' he said.

'You let me grieve for the life I should have had and for the person I should have been.'

And together, over the following weeks, they'd made a plan. They'd chosen a different life.

'I am not grieving,' he said.

'Okay,' she conceded. 'But did you ever think that maybe the past has caught up with me, too? That my dad—his betrayal, my past, *our* past— is something we should talk about? Something I need to talk about?'

'Your father was a fool.'

'My father led us here.'

'I came back to England for you—because of you. Not your father,' he denied. 'But this—the past—cannot impede our engagement announcement tonight.'

'But I *am* your past,' she said. 'How can you separate the two without confronting what that means?'

'It means nothing.'

Exasperated, she asked, 'Why is today so important to you?'

'Imagine eyes, hundreds of them, watching *you*, knowing *your* name and everything about you when you know nothing of them. Then imagine standing before them, waiting for them to accept you.'

'It must have been hard…' she whispered, scared for the boy he'd once been. Alone. Craving acceptance. She knew the bitter taste of rejection from those who should have accepted her unconditionally. Turning their backs on her. Betraying her.

'Under the command of the King they had to respect his wishes and accept me. Did they want me? Absolutely not. To them, I was a bastard. Raised by a whore who had shared in hedonistic delights with my father.' She physically recoiled from his words, and he quickly added, 'The truth is the truth and I will not hide from it.'

'But your mum…?' she gasped, not knowing what she wanted to ask, exactly, but knowing she wanted to defend her. While they'd been in care together Akeem had spoken of her with nothing but pure idolisation. These words now did not reflect the woman he'd loved.

'I was my mother's son, but I am my father's heir.' he explained cryptically.

She called him out. 'Was?' she asked. 'Not am?'

'She is dead.'

'So is my dad—but I'm still his daughter.'

Bearded jaw twitching, he regarded her with intense eyes before answering. 'I was a stranger to the Taliedaaen people, to their way of life and their struggles. Did they respect me? They had no choice. I am of royal blood, and rightful heir to the throne. Did they respect my mother?' he asked, and waited for her reply.

But she didn't have one.

'No,' he answered for her. 'She fled her home in shame. She had no power. No privilege,' he snarled, his lips folding back to reveal perfectly white teeth. 'Here in Taliedaa I am my father's heir, and they will respect you, Charlotte, because I will command it.'

'You will command it the way your father should have done for your mother?'

'This is nothing like that. Their relationship—'

'Your father and mum had a *relationship*?'

'Whatever they had,' he dismissed heavily, 'the people did not want her. They did not want me, but I need them to want *you*.'

'How do we do that?'

'By convincing them we are real. Not fire and passion, but stability and strength. Not pomp and heirs and titles but something else—something *real*. Something my father never offered to his people or his country. He offered them false promises. Nothing but mistress after mistress. As his Queen stayed hidden in her quarters until she died, childless. You will not be *that* kind of queen.'

Eyes wide, she stared. 'You want me to have a baby?'

'No!' he denied, the word vehement.

His eyes flashed and her stomach tugged.

'I need them to want change. Appreciable change. You are that change.'

'I am?'

'If I had sent you home after what my men saw, doubt would have shadowed me as I took my rule. This is the first step to showing them I will *not* rule as my father did. That pleasurable pursuits are not my aim. That the changes I suggest are for the good of the people, the country. Stable. Honest. Good.'

'Like your mum?' She didn't know where the question had come from, but here she was, asking it. Defending his mother. A stranger who'd given up her life in Taliedaa to raise Akeem in England. *That* was strength. Giving up everything she'd known for her family. Her son. A bit like her. Charlotte had given up everything for her family. Her dad.

His eyes flashed. 'My mother was defenceless—powerless in my father's world and in yours. I am neither of those things here.'

No, he was a vision of animated strength. 'But you think you were defenceless before? In England?' she asked, as the question formed in her mind. 'Powerless?'

He flinched—only slightly, but she saw it. The shudder. 'The boy I was when I was with you was weak, Charlotte. Unwanted.' His nostrils flared. 'Untamed.'

She'd wanted him, but the look in his eyes told her to keep that to herself, so she asked, 'Do you have something to prove because of your dad's actions? Or because of who you were before you were a prince?'

'Both,' he confirmed, and her heart broke a little for him. They were so similar and so different.

'A bit like me…' She tried to smile but her lips twisted uncomfortably. 'I have wasted so much time, and I have so much to prove, too.'

His face contorted. His full bottom lip flattening his jaw. 'I cannot let this—this need you have to compare our lives—get in the way. I need you to be—'

'To be the future Queen. And you'll be *him*?'

He frowned. 'Him?'

'The Crown Prince.'

'Who else?'

'Whoever came into this room.'

'*I* came in here,' he said.

No, he hadn't—but she kept her opinion to herself.

'You doubt it?' he asked, watching her face, her too-expressive eyes.

She couldn't lie. He'd know.

'I doubt nothing—I can feel it.'

'You're mistaken.'

'You're going to marry me,' she pushed. 'Won't you have to come to my room? Won't we share a bed? Or will I share a bed with *him*?'

'You'll share a bed with me, *qalbi*,' he promised, and moved towards her, towering over her with his scent, his heat. He stroked a finger across her cheek. 'The King.'

His scent was the same, but his presence...

'What if I don't want the King?' she asked boldly. 'What if I want the man on the plane... the man who came to my bedroom this morning?'

His wandering finger stopped its delicate tracing of her cheek to move to her chin. 'The King is all you will have, Lottie.' He tilted her face upwards, his eyes obsidian, boring into her. 'Because I *am* the King.'

He turned on his heel and didn't look back once as he closed the door behind him.

Lottie didn't want the King.

She wanted him.

Hadn't she always?

Collecting her shawl and sketchpad, she felt emotion hum through her. Because if all he could give her was a king, she'd be a queen-in-waiting he'd never expected.

And she knew just the woman to help her.

CHAPTER SEVEN

AKEEM'S SKIN TINGLED. The fine hairs on his arms rose to acknowledge her presence before he'd even seen her.

He turned, and saw that at the top of the stone steps someone had been delivered to him. But it was not *his* Charlotte. Not the girl with ripped tights and ill-fitting clothes.

His breath caught as one of her arms, covered in thin red lace down to her wrist, made contact with the stone balustrade.

She was a vision in cherry-red, with her hair curled around her face, and the candelabra positioned on top of the columns on either side of the staircase appeared to be for her own personal lighting. She glowed almost iridescently. The choker round her neck, its ruby feathering the dip below her throat, and the golden crown on her head, made her the perfect definition of what she presented herself to be.

A queen.

His eyes travelled down the length of her. From

the boat neckline, to the bodice pulled in at her waist by a simple satin bow, to the flaring skirts meeting her ankles. A red-covered foot took a step, and then another, as a feather-light touch guided her down the stairs.

She glided towards him. 'Will I do?'

He swallowed thickly. 'Will you *do*?'

It was clear, from the crown in her hair to her carefully painted lips and her elegantly fitted shoes—which brought her almost to his height, lips to lips—that this Charlotte was...*different*. She'd been transformed...*for him*.

His hand moved to her waist. 'You will do,' he said, and no god, and certainly no man, would have believed he'd spent all day trying to forget going to her room...spent all day remembering who he was and who he'd become.

Because here it was—everything he didn't want.

Passion.

Plush lips hovered just in front of his. She didn't kiss him, simply kept her mouth just within reach, letting a hint of her sweetness and warmth seep into him.

He cleared his throat, breaking the invisible magic holding them in each other's aura, and pushed down those feelings of inadequacy that had haunted him his entire life. The reason he'd believed Charlotte's father so easily.

He held out his hand and offered it to her. 'Ready?'

A memory of the last time he'd asked her if she was ready pulled at his insides. He would not entertain it. Not now.

Straightening her spine, she exhaled a silent breath through pursed lips. 'Ready,' she said, and slid her hand into his.

He felt it then. The slight tremble. Was it him, or was it her? He didn't know, so he didn't acknowledge it.

He inclined his head, and the staff who'd been invisible before moved in front of them and swept open the double doors to the formal reception room which led to the royal balcony. They stepped inside, perfectly in sync. But he didn't see the surrounding room, or the staff standing beside the doors to the balcony, waiting for his signal that they were ready.

His heart hammered. There, on that same balcony, his father had forced his people to accept him, the illegitimate son of the King. Now he was going to demand they accept his Queen.

His Charlotte.

'Akeem, you're hurting me.'

His heart remembered to beat, flushing blood through his veins in a tidal wave. He looked down at the hand beneath his and instantly loosened his hold. 'I'm sorry.'

His head swam with all the words they'd

shared since London. All the angry words and unexpected confessions. His throat was tight, his mouth dry.

'Ready?' she whispered, a gentle smile tugging at her full lips.

Was he? Was he ready to put his past in front of his future? To give it a place? A home?

He nodded, feeling a tightness pulling at his cheekbones. He gave the signal. A long blink of his too-wide eyes.

Slowly, the black wooden doors opened onto the city below. His desert kingdom. He entwined his fingers in hers, resisting the urge to bring her hand to his mouth and place a kiss on the back of it. To reassure her that everything was going to be fine. It would be. He'd make sure of it. But he did not want to put doubt into her smile, nor into the confident presence holding his hand. He did not want to acknowledge the hand of doubt pressing down on his sternum.

Stepping forward onto the balcony, he kept her hand in his. Kept her near as he looked at his people, standing toe to toe with nobility and dignitaries, as cameras recorded this moment when the Crown Prince would reveal his bride.

Their future Queen.

His gaze worked over the crowd that filled the palace gardens. More trailed out of the enormous gates and down the mountainside. He did not smile. He pulled Charlotte towards him, into his side, and inclined his head.

The crowd erupted.

Cheers.

Akeem raised his hand and the excitement instantly stilled. He opened his mouth to speak, but it was not his own voice he heard.

It was hers.

'*Shukran...*' She spoke clearly, as if trained to make her voice move over each face in the crowd. 'Thank you,' she repeated in English. And then, slow and choppy, she continued in his mother tongue.

In his mother tongue.

'In time, I hope to be as crucial as the rubies mined at the northern border, in the valley of Dalah, where the Dead Sea gifts life. As valuable as the emeralds from the south and the gold mined right here in Taliedaa. Because I intend to mirror those jewels.'

She licked at her lower lip.

'I will serve you, the people of Taliedaa, by spending my time amongst you, offering support and comfort to your future King.' She turned to him then, and the green of her eyes was as vibrant as those minerals mined by his people. 'The Crown Prince,' she said. 'The future. The rightful heir to Taliedaa's throne.'

She bowed to him, dipping her chin to her chest.

Applause.

A sense of restlessness itched at his skin and locked his jaw. *Regret.* It ate at him. He'd tricked her by seducing her with the word 'closure', and now here she was...the perfect Queen for an imperfect king.

He raised her up and pulled her to him, leant down and brushed his mouth against hers. A touch of softness. Of warmth. Of her *presence.* There it was—duty's kiss. Mouth to mouth, lip to lip. Perfunctory.

But it didn't feel perfunctory.

It felt powerful.

He wasn't alone.

There was someone on his side. Standing with him—*for* him.

No one had ever been on his side. Yes, he'd stood with his father on this balcony, but they'd been separate entities. Standing only for themselves. In the group pictures at the children's home he had been one of many, but they had been alone. Apart. On different journeys. And in the foster families... He'd never been with them long enough to stand with them—to be a part of what they were. *Family.* But here, with her—in front of his people...

He moved back, his hands still in hers, and stared at her. He'd ripped her from her life, thrust her into his, and she had sold the lie that this marriage was something real because he'd asked her to.

She'd made the people want her.

Want change.

And she'd done it for him.

For so long he'd pushed for change—to bring the best and be the best for his people—and now Charlotte had gone above and beyond to help him succeed.

He couldn't have done it without her. Not so swiftly. The roars of applause had never been so genuine. His country needed a queen.

He needed a Charlotte.

He turned to his people once more and raised their hands.

And so the cheers rang again.

Acceptance.

But her words from this morning clawed at him.

'Did you ever think that maybe the past has caught up with me, too? That my dad, his betrayal, my past—our past—is something we should talk about? Something I need to talk about?'

She was right. He should have considered it. Her need to talk. He owed her for his. To listen. To treat her like a human being and be decent.

He gripped her elbow, and after a deep inclination of his head and chest he turned them away from the crowds still cheering.

He would listen now.

The enormous doors closed behind them on their iron hinges. Akeem gently removed his fingers from her elbow and walked further into the room, leaving her staring at the broad expanse of his back covered by a black outer cloak.

Adrenaline pumped through her. 'What's wrong?' she asked. 'Did I do something wrong?'

He turned. His dark eyes were luminous beneath the white scarf feathering his cheeks. He held a finger to his lips and the gold-tipped sleeve fell back to reveal a thick wrist. Her eyes followed the golden seam to his black inner robes. She bit her lip, waiting for the staff to leave as he dismissed them.

'There *is* a problem,' he confirmed when they were alone.

Tension gripped her. 'Problem?'

He pointed a long, steady finger at her chest. 'You made the crown fit,' he continued, 'and became a queen. You did everything right.'

'Then what is it?'

He dropped his hand. 'If this is going to work…'

His eyes travelled from the crown pinned in her hair, over her carefully made-up face, to the choker at her throat. She burned wherever his eyes lingered.

'We need to be alone. Completely.'

She raised a brow. 'What for?'

'To talk.'

'Who will talk?' she asked, wrinkling her nose.

'You.'

'What do you want me to talk about?'

'You said you wanted to talk this morning.'

'I did?'

'You said I should have considered that you need to,' he reminded her. 'I have considered.'

'And what did you decide?'

'That if you need to talk, I will listen.'

'Because you want to?'

'Because we need to get to know each other again.'

'What do you mean, *"get to know each other"*?' she asked, wrinkling her nose. 'I'm in a better dress...' She fisted the fabric at her waist and pulled it out. 'But underneath it's me.'

'And who *is* that?' he asked, his face unreadable. 'The girl I knew couldn't have been like *that* out there.'

'Been like what?'

'Perfect.'

She wrung her hands together in front of her. 'Selma helped me,' she explained, her throat clogged. 'She helped me craft what I wanted to say. What I wanted to project to your people.'

His eyes narrowed. 'And what did you want to project?'

'Myself,' she husked. Because that was all she'd ever wanted to project. 'Here, in your country, I can be all the things my dad said I couldn't be. And all the bad things—' she grimaced '—I believed about myself, I can lock in a box and throw away the key, can't I? Push it under the bed and only keep the good things. The parts of myself that make me *me*.'

He didn't move. Didn't contradict her. He stared at her. 'If this is going to work,' he said again, 'I want to understand the person you have become. I want to know the why and the how. Who you were and who you are now.' He extended his hand. 'Let us know each other again, *qalbi*.'

She didn't know who moved forward, but her awareness of his fingers sliding between hers was explosive. *Intensity.* It was always there—even out there on the balcony. His lips had pressed against hers in the most chaste of kisses. But the first kiss after the plane had not been a kiss from a king. It had been a kiss from Akeem.

And she would find him again.

'Where will we go?'

'Every palace has its secrets,' he said, running a hand through his hair. 'I will show you mine.'

But would he show her as the man or the King?

CHAPTER EIGHT

'WHAT IS THIS?' Charlotte smoothed her fingers over a carving that resembled a flower. She turned to him, the gravel crunching beneath her feet. 'Is it a tomb?'

'No.'

'A dungeon?'

'It is neither of those things.'

She squinted at the primitive entrance. It had to be a tunnel. 'A cave?'

Something clicked above her right ear and she turned to him.

'We both need a little magic,' he said, holding out a long wooden stick for her inspection.

'The magic of fire?' Her nose wrinkled. 'Mankind discovered fire long before our times.'

He raised it above their heads and ignited a flame. 'There is more,' he promised, and caught her hand.

She gasped as, with a powerful arm around her waist, he pulled her inside with him.

She couldn't see a thing.

'The first and only time my father brought me down here,' he told her as he moved in front of her to lead the way, 'he left me here in the dark.'

'Why would he do that?'

Akeem sneered. 'To see if I could find my way back.'

'Did you?'

'I did,' he said. 'But not before I found something else first.'

'It's so dark… I'm surprised you found anything,' she whispered. 'I can barely see my own hands. There's nothing here but rock.'

'Look with better eyes, *qalbi*.'

'I can see…' She squinted. 'Rock.'

'Look further than the end of your nose.'

'But that's the safest place to look when you can only plan your next step.'

'Is that what life has been like for you?' he asked. 'Only planning the next step?'

'I thought what my life has been like was easy for you to figure out?'

'It was,' he said. 'But I want to know the why— the how.'

'That's not a simple thing to answer…' she said, and suddenly the past became too visceral, the hunger she could never sate pulling at her abdomen. 'I just did it.'

'Did what?'

'Survived, of course.'

He stopped in front of her. His eyes still on the

path ahead, he said, 'Then let there be more light, *qalbi*, so you can plan your next step better.'

He placed his torch on the cave wall, and as the flame caught and blazed its heat was transferred to the lamp next to it, and the next, until all around them lights raged like fireflies.

Akeem threw the torch into a corner. Pre-prepared kindling lit up like a furnace in aceramic bowl, and just as the flames had kissed each other to rage into light, so did the ceramic pots buried in the ground. All around them was light, where before there had been none, coming to life around them, from deep within the red earth, one flame after another.

The red stone walls burst into life around them, bringing the cavern and a natural pool to life. The waters, so still and so blue, became almost translucent before them. Unexpected lush green and foliage climbed the walls.

Shadows and flame had turned the darkness into something living. Something oozing life. Left by the generations before them who had passed through here.

It was an oasis underground.

She moved to stand beside him. 'It's beautiful.'

And it was. It was almost alien in its beauty. And its unexpectedness overwhelmed her with its utter abundance of life—so much alive and living where it shouldn't. She felt so small before it. So insignificant.

'This reminds me to be better,' he said, his eyes forward. 'Bigger.'

'I feel it,' she replied. 'Something bigger… something more…' Filling her lungs with a fortifying breath full of heat, burning wood, and the scent of death and life, she said, 'I was always scared I'd never become something bigger. Something *more*.'

'More?' He turned to her. 'More what?'

'I used to think there was only one type of "more". More money to pay the bills so I would never see a red bill again. That would bring me peace. More food so I could have a full fridge and feel full…content. More clothes so I'd feel warm, and—' The word *loved* was on the tip of her tongue. She stopped herself. 'I believed that more…' she searched for the words '… more physical things would bring me to a place of happiness. But after these last few nights in the palace…'

His face twisted into a mangling of harsh lines. 'The palace wasn't enough?'

'The palace was plenty,' she soothed. 'But I haven't slept well there,' she confessed.

'Why not?'

'The sheets are so soft.'

'And…?' he asked.

'The sheets are so soft I can't sleep,' she clarified. 'Not because they're uncomfortable, but because comfort itself is very new to me. I haven't been comfortable. *Ever*. I'm afraid of it.' Her eyes turned large. 'A few days ago I buried my father. I was facing eviction, and the prospect of throwing myself on the mercy of the benefits system.'

'What does this have to do with anything?' he asked.

'It has *everything* to do with everything. Because after talking with you this morning…' She trailed off. This morning felt like another life, not a few hours ago. She started again. 'After talking with you I realised the "more" I wanted was inside. I needed to believe I was worthy enough to accept the quality of fine cotton sheets.'

'And do you believe it now?'

She held his gaze. 'I've never believed it. That I am worthy of more. Worthy of the things others took for granted. I was always on the outside, waiting to be let in. Nobody wanted to be friends with a girl whose dad roamed the streets with a can of lager and stumbled and fell into people's gardens.' She wanted to close her eyes, but the intensity of his held her fast. 'I'm still afraid. *Inside*. That the world will only ever recognise me as his daughter.'

Akeem remained silent. Still. So very still. 'Why?'

'My dad…' Her eyes grew hot. 'He never loved me. He told me. Told me he could never love something he'd made because it was in my genes—in my DNA—to fail. Like he had at everything. And if he couldn't love me, his own daughter, how could anyone else?'

'Charlotte…'

'I was determined to make him live. Determined not to fail my father.' She closed her eyes tightly. 'I was determined to make him live and I failed him.'

There—she'd said it. The whole truth. Why she was so adamant that here she would be more. Would be all the things she'd promised herself she would be until her dad had told her she wasn't capable. He had convinced her that she was his daughter and therefore destined to fail. And in the end she had failed. He'd died because the one time he'd needed her, she hadn't been there.

'You failed no one,' Akeem said quietly.

She opened her eyes and met his. He was watching her intensely. 'I did,' she corrected.

'Charlotte—'

'So, yes….' She cut him off. 'I'm still afraid, but I'm no longer scared to try. I'm not scared of being here. I'm not scared of this, or of cotton sheets. I'm not afraid to live any more. I will not live my life in the shadows, in fear of failing— like my dad.'

Closing the space between them with a purposeful stride, he kissed her. Her eyelids first. Then her cheeks.

'Our brief whirlwind affair,' she said, 'was the best time and the worst time of my life. The worst was when social services came and found my dad drunk on the sofa, the house empty of food. They

took me into care at the children's home because
I had nowhere else to go. Then I met you.'

'And?'

'And you were everything.' A trembling smile
tugged at her lips. 'Strong. Resilient. But most of
all you didn't care where I'd come from—*who* I'd
come from,' she corrected. 'You were kind. You
showed me the ropes in an environment I never
thought I'd be in. No one had ever helped me before. No one had ever helped me to survive.'

'I remember giving you a sketchpad and pencils.'

'And I spent all my time drawing you.' She
smiled. 'When I got to go home, and we made all
those plans to leave when you turned eighteen,
I believed that there was more—that I could be
more. That I was worthy of a different life. A better life. That I was enough. But after you disappeared it was easier to believe my dad's version of
my life. Because you'd left me behind. Because in
the end I hadn't been worth the trouble. I hadn't
been enough for the one person who'd made me
question how I was living my life.'

'It was not the truth.'

His words scraped at her skin. It would be all
too easy to fall back into the heavy ache of worth-
lessness that had been an unwavering constant
throughout her life. But his eyes held fast to hers.
Locking her into him. Into the moment.

'I didn't know that,' she said. 'I was sixteen—

you were the only person to make me question my life. To convince me there was more out there.'

He laughed—a gentle sound. 'I only showed you where to find the best cereal in the communal kitchen.'

'You showed me there was more,' she corrected him. 'That I could *be* more. If I took a chance the way you were taking a chance. You were leaving the children's home behind and you were determined to learn your trade as a labourer, so one day you could build skyscrapers in the sky.'

'And instead I became this.'

'Is this life better?' she asked. 'Being the son of a king?'

Deep lines appeared in the smooth skin between his eyes. 'Yes.'

'Why?'

He smiled. 'Why is it better?'

'Yes… You said your dad was selfish?' She grimaced when his eyes shot flames, as if trying to incinerate her line of questioning. But she wanted to know. 'I want to know what it was like for you,' she said. 'Were you afraid of coming here?' she asked. 'Afraid that they—the people—would only see a boy in care?'

'I was angry,' he confessed. 'Angry with you, with your father, and most of all with my father.' He shook his head. 'There was too much rage for me to be frightened.'

'What did he say?'

'Who?'

'Your dad,' she replied. 'Did you confront him about your mum?'

'You do not confront a king.'

'But you're a prince—his son.'

'All he saw when he looked at me was his legacy being continued. If I had questions—needs—there were other people for that.'

'But you were so much more than that.'

'Was I?'

'Yes! You were a little boy who'd got left behind. A boy who turned himself into a capable young man.'

'My father needed an heir,' he interjected. 'Not the boy I was or the man I was becoming.'

'What about family?' Her heart broke for him. 'You were his *son*.'

'I was an illegitimate bastard,' he corrected her, and she recoiled from the hatred in his voice. 'I was nothing. I came from nothing. And he did not let me forget it.'

Her mouth flew open. 'You came from him and your mum. You came from love.'

'I came from the swapping of bodily fluids. I was a child who'd grown up in a foreign land, in a system that did not grow men—it broke them.'

'You were not broken,' she whispered. 'How?' she asked, rage heating her cheeks. 'How did he not let you forget?'

'There was a contract...'

'A *contract*?'

'I had to forget the man and become the Prince. Become Crown Prince Akeem Abd al-Uzza and leave Akeem Ali where he belonged. He made me change my name. He made me—'

'Put him away in a box? He made you put who you were in a box? Like you told me to do with my feelings. Hide them. Shove them out of sight. Forget them.'

His nostrils flared. 'Something like that.'

'No,' she corrected. 'Not "something like that". That was it, wasn't it? Like my dad... Oh, my God. He made you feel exactly like my dad did when you came to the house. Like a monster.' She covered her mouth, holding in the scream gurgling in her throat. 'He made you feel like everything you were was ugly. Bad. Destined to fail. Like my dad.'

'He did not make me feel like that,' he denied. 'He made me a king.'

'No, you did that on your own,' she corrected. 'You never would have failed—with or without him.'

'I do not believe you're scared any more,' he said. Deflecting her.

She let him.

'Why not?' she husked.

'You were fearless on the balcony,' he replied. 'And you are fearless now.'

Fearless? A lightness fluttered through her.

She stilled. 'I may not have chosen to be here, Akeem, but I can choose who I am. Who I want to be.'

'And you want to be the woman on the balcony?' he asked.

'I want to be myself.'

'Yourself?' he repeated. 'And who is that?'

'I'm not sure,' she said, a hesitant smile on her lips. 'But I'm excited to find out.'

'On the balcony you were a queen, and in here you are—'

'A woman?'

'Yes…'

'I can be both and still me.'

'It is not possible to be two people in one body.'

'Not two people,' she corrected. 'Only one. I'm not hiding one part of myself in favour of another.' She stilled. 'Is that what you do? Split yourself? Show your people the King you were out there and conceal this man, hiding in the dark with me?'

He didn't answer. Instead, he stared at her with an intensity she'd never seen before. He lowered his head and crushed his mouth against hers. Kissed her so hard he drowned out the voices in her head. The doubting voices. The voice of her dad. Just the way he had almost a decade ago. He'd listened to her, to every word she'd had to say. He'd seen her. And now he knew what she needed, just as he'd known when he'd taken her to his hiding place at St John's. Behind the tree.

Except this time she didn't need to be soothed. She needed to be touched. Touched by him. Set on fire as she burned the parts of her past she no longer needed in his arms and kept only the parts she wanted.

His mouth pushed hard against hers, his tongue pushing through the barriers of her lips to stroke at the insides of her mouth. It would be easy to let herself fall into the pleasure he was offering her, to resist the knowledge of what he was doing. But she couldn't.

She didn't want him to hide from the past. From hers or his. Because it had made them and this moment possible. It deserved acknowledgement.

She twisted free, her hands on his chest. She pushed away. 'Are you trying to hide, Akeem?'

'I am standing firmly between your legs, *qalbi*,' he said, and backed her up against the wall.

He was lying. She could feel it. The distance.

His mouth moved down, kiss by kiss, until he met her hardening nipple. He closed his mouth around the bud, sucking her and the fabric into his mouth.

Charlotte closed her eyes and let him run. He hadn't run away from the intensity like he had this morning. He was falling into it. Into her. But still she felt that distance. His refusal to acknowledge the boy she'd known.

As as he ran, so did she. She ran from the past, from the present, to be right there in his arms. *In the moment.* Alive and living. She let herself enjoy the pressure of his mouth on her.

The cave wall was hard against her back, but she didn't care.

This was life.

She had chosen life.

Her fingers slipped into the hair at the base of his head and she moaned. Low and deep.

'Oh…' Her hands reached for his shoulders, holding on as need ravaged through her. 'Oh, my…'

He stroked his fingers firmly down the valley between her breasts, to the bodice of her dress where the skirts flared out. Her insides throbbed as he put his hand beneath her skirt and trailed his fingers up the length of her leg, to graze gently against the fleshy inside of her thigh.

He put his fingers to her core, moving over her centre in a tantalising swipe. 'Do you want me to touch you here, Charlotte?'

'Yes,' she said. 'God, yes, I do.'

He didn't hesitate. He swiped her panties aside, pressing his fingers down along the wet folds of her to part her sex and open her up to him. He thrust a finger inside her.

Her core clenched around it. *'Akeem!'*

'I know my name,' he told her, and eased another finger inside her. Everything tensed—pulled tight like a stretched elastic band.

She looked up into his face, everything in her

body urging her to bear down on his hand. 'Do you?' she husked. Did he even know that the man between her legs was not the Crown Prince?

He didn't answer. Deft fingers undid the choker at her throat and it fell to their feet. Charlotte didn't hear the tear of fabric, only felt the heat of his mouth on her. He moved down her throat, sucking and nipping as he came to her breast. His free hand tugged down the red lace covering her breasts and bared them to him. The hard nubs were waiting for him to claim them. He sucked, bringing a nipple deep into his mouth, and feathered his tongue over the tight bud.

Her hands dived from his shoulders to his hair, pushing and digging their nails into his scalp. He worked her body, her flesh. An explosive need made her push down on to his hand, seeking more, seeking friction.

'Please…' she begged.

Please, please, please, she wanted to say, because it was his word now. It belonged to him. It was only his face she saw. He was the only one she would ever beg for release.

And he didn't deny her.

He pushed another finger inside her, imitating what she wanted him to do with the bigger and harder length of him pushing against her stomach.

'Oh, my!'

He answered by pressing more deeply inside her, his fingers sliding smoothly in and out and his thumb moving against her in a hypnotic circling motion. She moaned into his mouth, giving herself up to the pleasure, to the feel of him against her and his fingers between her thighs.

'I...' She closed her eyes. She was too many sensations. Too much everything. She reached for him. 'I want to touch you.'

She moved her hands over his shoulders, over the taut muscles of his back. His chest. Lower.

He caught her wrist. 'No.'

The pad of his thumb moved over her clitoris and he leaned into her, keeping her trapped between the wall and the hardness of him.

'I want to touch you,' she pleaded. She ached to touch him. To bring him the pleasure he was bringing her.

The tempo of his fingers increased. 'I've dreamt of this moment for too long to find release at your touch like an inexperienced teen,' he answered, his voice dry and hoarse. His words weren't a compliment, but a statement—a breathless sentiment acknowledging his need.

Her body grew tight with the thrum of his fingers. She couldn't help it. She said, 'Then don't. I want you inside me.'

The noise that left his mouth was half roar, half battle cry. He pulled his fingers out of her with a quickness that caught at her breath. He grabbed her by the hips and picked her up, pushing her against the wall until the hardest part of him, still concealed by his trousers, pushed at her centre.

'When I take you,' he told her. 'When I push myself inside you because you beg for me—and you *will* beg,' he promised. 'It will not be against a stone wall. It will be in a bed. My bed.'

His tongue plundered her mouth and he rocked against her. Harder. Faster.

She screamed. 'Akeem!' His name was a plea. A gasp, a moan—a guttural cry of need. It was animalistic to her own ears. A primal call for her mate. Her secret confessions hadn't made her feel uncomfortable, she recognised. They had set a primitive part of herself free... And Akeem needed to confront his past too, not hide it, or he'd never be able to let it go as he'd instructed her to do.

He was hiding his true self in plain sight. He was hiding behind the version of him that was the future King. But this Akeem, bringing her pleasure and ignoring his own... This Akeem listening to her tales of woe because he wanted to, because he wanted to know her... *This* was the Akeem she wanted to know.

The man of fire and passion between her legs. *Her* Akeem.

The Akeem she'd known...the Akeem she knew still.

He pushed harder, grinding against her throbbing core and taking her to an edge she'd never leant over. A pulsing, electrifying edge.

'Come for me, Charlotte.'

Her body tightened, her nails clawing into Akeem's shoulders as convulsion after trembling convulsion burst through her and tore her apart.

She sagged against him and splintered into a million pieces. He stilled, and she couldn't stop trembling.

He was so warm against her. Hard. But there was a softness in the hands holding her to him. Shielding her...protecting her as she came back down from the heights of ecstasy. And it was all too easy to let him hold her up.

Maybe, when they found this bed of his, she could set Akeem free, too.

What was she doing to him? He'd dry-humped his future Queen against a wall. The thought of pushing inside her—filling her with himself—had almost undone him.

She smiled up at him and it crushed him. He couldn't smile back.

He'd lost control, and she'd given him permission to do it. To give in to the carnal urges driving him. He was everything his father had told him he was.

Primitive.

He'd destroyed her dress. Ripped the seams to expose her red lace-covered breasts.

He lowered her gently to her feet and shrugged the outer cloak from his body and wrapped it around her shoulders. He moulded his hands over her. Over the reality of her shoulders.

He needed her to understand.

He caught her chin. 'Who are you?' he asked.

He had to make her understand what he'd failed to make her believe nine years ago, because he'd been weak and believed her father. Someone needed to believe in her, and first it had to be herself, but he would guide her on her way as no one had guided him.

He owed her this small gift. A gift she'd given to the boy he could never be again.

'Charlotte,' she said. She moistened her lips with the tip of her tongue. 'Who else could I be?'

'Tell me who you are.'

'Charlotte...' It was a murmur this time, confusion narrowing her eyes.

'Charlotte who?' he demanded.

'Charlotte Hegarty.'

'Say it again.'

'I am—' She inhaled deeply.

The smell of burning wood and the heat of their mingled arousal infiltrated his senses as he watched a veil lift from her eyes.

'I'm Charlotte Hegarty.'

'And Charlotte Hegarty is enough.' He pulled her to him and lifted her against him, pressed her firmly to his heaving chest. 'Charlotte Hegarty is worthy of more than high-quality cotton sheets.'

A hiccup of a sound left her lips. Not a laugh... not a moan or a gasp. 'And are *you* worthy of top-of-the-range sheets?'

'I have never denied myself comfort.'

'You've denied me at every opportunity,' she husked, and his heart raged, along with the harder, pulsing length of him.

No, he'd denied himself.

'Did I not give you release? Pleasure?'

'What about *your* pleasure?'

'If I'd torn the panties from your body and thrust myself inside you...possessed you... I would have been everything my father told me I was. A basic boy, with basic needs and basic desires.'

'There was nothing basic about what we just did, Akeem,' she said gently. Too gently.

But she was wrong.

He would have been nothing but flesh and hard muscle finding release. That was *basic* at its core definition. The impulse of the man who had driven to London to exact his revenge would have taken over. An impulse he could not give life to in this world.

He would have been a pleasure-seeker at the cost of others. At the cost of Charlotte. He had no protection with him, and if his seed had taken root inside her—made a life because he hadn't been able to control himself...

'Can you tell me your name?' she asked, and his face contorted.

He was nothing but a name now. Nothing but his blood. Nothing but his kingdom. He had one name, and she knew it.

'I am Akeem Abd al-Uzza, Crown Prince of Taliedaa. The only heir by blood to the Taliedaaen throne,' he answered. Because that was the only person he could be. Even down here, with the world nowhere to be seen, no one to see them. Because it didn't matter if they couldn't see them. *He* would know.

'Is he worthy?' she asked, and he sucked in a sharp inhalation of air. He'd been trying to prove his worth as the chosen Crown Prince for nine years.

'We claim our own worth, *qalbi*,' he answered truthfully. Because that was what he was trying to do now—claim it by proving it. By not being his father or the boy he'd once been.

'I'm so glad you've claimed yours, Akeem,' she said. 'I'm so glad the boy I knew found his place, despite his father and mine. Despite St John's... I'm so glad that, despite it all, he found his *home*.'

She breathed the word 'home', and the word felt distant. Alien. He lived within the palace walls. He ruled a kingdom. The desert was in his genes. But was it *home*?

Home was belonging. Acceptance.

He had neither.

He steeled himself against her words about belonging. *That* boy had never found his place—his home…

'The world told him there was no home for a boy like him,' she continued. 'His father told him that everything he was, he didn't care for. And you proved them all wrong. You did it, Akeem, and your mother would be proud of you. Of that boy.'

Her words were a knife in his heart. All he'd done was for her. His mother. To make her sacrifices worth it.

He choked back words and tugged Charlotte into him. Lifting her effortlessly against him, he moved towards the exit.

Her hands around his neck, she leant into the crook of his neck and said sleepily. 'I can walk.'

'Shush,' he soothed, because he needed her against him, needed her presence…because he was raw, electrified and stripped to the bone. He had not felt this disjointed since his arrival in Taliedaa.

It had been a mistake to bring her here. He hurried back the way he'd come, carrying Charlotte tightly against him. He'd brought no one here. He'd exposed himself. Revealed the secrets to his survival. And now every time he came here to remind himself to be better…stronger…he would see her face…

He did not want to feel. *Not this.* This pure, undiluted desire and a need, as she had said, for more…

There was going to come a time when he wouldn't be able to distract her with sex. She'd want him to share himself, and she'd keep asking questions because it was her nature…

What would she do when he couldn't answer? When she found out that the boy she kept pushing him to show her was dead?

CHAPTER NINE

ROUGHLY, CHARLOTTE SMUDGED the pad of her thumb against the sketch, to blend the thicker lines of charcoal into lighter tones. She was attempting to draw his hands. The hands that had held her against that wall. The hands that he had used to turn her on and melt her bones so mercilessly. The hands that belonged to Akeem. The man who wouldn't show himself to her. The man she wanted desperately to remember that he was more than a dutiful king.

The servants had brought an easel last night, and a trolley to keep her art supplies on, and it had been...*wonderful*. Making lines and smudges, expressing herself—

'Lottie.'

Hurriedly, she flipped her drawing over and turned to face the doorway. Akeem stood there, wearing white loose-fitting trousers and a long tunic.

'Still not ready?' he asked, and a guilty flush heated her cheeks.

'No, it's not ready.'

'You weren't so shy before.'

'It's been a long time.' She brushed off her hands. Trying to free her fingertips of soot. 'I'm feeling my way back in.'

'I have something that will help.'

'What is it?'

He stepped closer to her. 'Come with me and I'll show you.'

'Where?' she asked, her body all too aware of his approach. His closeness.

'It's a surprise.'

She arched a brow. 'More caves?'

He laughed and pointed. 'You have charcoal on your nose.'

She didn't laugh back. She placed her charcoal on to her new art trolley and stood. This was her chance.

'I'll come with you,' she said, reaching for the watch at her wrist and unbuckling it with trembling fingers, 'if you tell me about this?'

She held it out to him. He stopped moving and she felt it. The distance he immediately put between them.

'What is there to tell?' He frowned. 'My mother tied that watch around my wrist on my first day at school and reclaimed it when she collected me. She gave it to me and retrieved it every day until she couldn't. That is it. That's the story.'

'No.' Her bare feet soundless, she moved closer. 'They're the facts.'

'There is no story. You asked me to tell you and I have.' He reached for her. 'Now we leave.'

She evaded him. 'What about the boy she left with it around his wrist every day? What about the boy who kept it? I want to know the *why*...' she repeated his words back at him '...the *how.*'

His expression controlled and unreadable, he replied, 'It is what it is.'

'Instinct?' she said, recalling her words to him last night. 'He survived, didn't he?' Her heart squeezed for the little boy he had been. Alone in his grief. Her eyes filled with unexpected tears.

'I guess he did,' he replied, his eyes sharp, watching her face, her expression.

'It must have been hard, surviving on your own for so long. With only this...' She looked down at the watch and swallowed down the lump in her throat.

His expression turned from passive to enraged. 'We both know you were as alone as I was.' His bearded cheek pulsed. 'We both survived.' His black eyes flashed. 'On our own.'

The past came hurtling back to her. 'Are you still surviving?' she asked.

'What do you mean?'

'Since I arrived you've used mechanisms... places where you hide.'

'I am right in front of you.'

'Yes, you are,' she said, 'but you pull away every time I get close. Last night you pulled away...' she shifted uneasily '...in your head.'

She made herself stand still. She wanted him to know, so she told him.

'You ran away.'

'I ran straight to you.'

She shook her head. 'You distracted me and I let you, because I understand running...'

She stalled, thinking about the right words—the right way to tell him that she got it. That she understood it—*him*—better now.

She swallowed. 'I understand how hard it is to let anyone close, because it's scary. Scary to think someone might *see* you. I let you see me last night, because I think we could be a family, Akeem.'

Eyes narrowed, he scoffed, 'A *family*?'

'If not a family...at least we could be friends.'

'Friends do not feel what we feel. They do not feel this intensity—'

'We're going to get married. We can choose what we are, can't we?'

His face gave nothing away, but his hands moved, his thumbs and forefingers grinding against one another at his hips.

'I was alone growing up with Dad,' she admitted. 'Glossing over that—what growing up with him was truly like—is a habit that isn't easily broken. But I want to stop glossing over it. Because telling you set a part of me free.'

She stopped talking for a moment, because she wasn't sure she was making sense.

'It will take time to get my dad's voice out of

my head…telling me to keep quiet,' she continued. 'But I don't have to be quiet any more.' She inhaled deeply. 'And neither do you.'

'Our marriage benefits the crown. The people.'

'It will still be a marriage,' she insisted. 'Two people who should be honest with each other. When one wants to run—the other runs with them. Catches them up and tells them they're worthy. When I ran in the cave, you caught me and told me I was enough…'

And, oh, how those words had moved her. It was the first time she'd ever heard them. But she shook it off. Right now, it wasn't about her. It was about him. The man who kept coming back to her. In London, to her bedroom … He had something to say, and she wanted to hear it.

'We made a deal,' she said. 'And now we need to make the deal work. So next time you want to run, Akeem, I'm going to run with you—because whether or not you like it, you might have bargained on getting yourself a temporary queen, but you got me too. A temporary family. So run all you like, but I'll catch you. Because that's what friends do. What *family* does.'

'Why is it so important to catch me, *qalbi*?' he asked, taking back the control he needed, when his urge was to run.

She'd tied her long hair back, and he wanted to release it. Set her curls free until they feathered her waist and the dip in her spine. He longed to explore with more than his hands...

'You have told me how—why—you have become *this* Charlotte,' he continued, 'but you did not tell me why you're helping me?'

'You didn't give me a choice, remember?'

She smiled. That small, knowing smile. He wasn't running. He was walking slowly towards her. Slackening the tension on that rope.

'There are always choices,' he said—because there were. He could have decided to be a no one. Instead, he'd become this. And he'd made the right choice.

Had she?

He raised his brow, his heart giving a painful double beat. 'A diploma?'

'I can do that on my own,' she dismissed, too easily. 'Why are you changing the subject? Stop deflecting.'

'I'm not deflecting.' *He was.* 'Tell me why?'

Another step. And there it was again. The stray bullet. Her presence. Her scent. He couldn't help it. He reached out, grasped her by the back of her neck, felt his knuckles cushioned by her curls, and reached up to remove the tie in her hair. It tumbled, heavy and long, around her face. He pulled her towards him.

'Why are you helping me?' he asked, and his eyes flicked to the pulse pumping hard at her throat. His lips thinned, and he answered for her. *'Kindness?'* It was a sneer, because it disgusted him.

The King did not need kindness. The King did not need the emotions tied to family or friends. Because emotions had no place in royal life. His father had administered that lesson, but *he* had put the teachings into practice. *He* had decided long ago that to be a true ruler he would set aside the part of himself that needed answers to the question *why*, because his destiny was to repair a broken legacy—not to weep over his mother or the love his father had denied him.

He didn't need to know why they'd abandoned him any more because he wasn't that boy. He was a king. *The* King.

But here she was, offering help anyway.

'No, not kindness,' she rejected. 'I knew a boy once who became a prince,' she said. 'I didn't see him for a really long time. I owe that boy a great debt, because he showed me once that there was another way to live. He gave me sanctuary, and when I lost him I forgot there could be another way.'

'And now?'

'The debt stands. I understand that now. I understand it wasn't his fault,' she continued. 'I stood still because of *me*. It was *my* fault. And now I hope I can move forward.'

'With the boy?' His voice was deep, the words low, conflicted.

'With the boy and the Prince,' she answered. 'One and the same, he told me. But the Prince also told me he could never really be the boy again, because he'd had to become someone else. Some-*thing* else. But I think he can be that boy again. I think he can be both. And I would like to meet them in the same skin, breathing the same air and in the same room.'

'I'm not the person you seek. This is not a fairy tale. There are no transformations at midnight—no toads to be kissed, no princes to rescue.'

'You can be the boy with *me*,' she said, ignoring him.

He could never be that boy again.

'The boy is weak.'

'And the King is strong?'

'The King has power, respect. The boy knew neither.'

'You're going to kiss me now, aren't you?'

'Yes.'

And he did.

He ran straight into the warmth of her body. Her kindness. And he closed off the voice in his ears telling him he wasn't worthy of friends—family. That he was weak for wanting them. Because he was starting to wonder if it was wrong.

He was distracting her again. Asking her lips to accept the thrust of his tongue and moving his hands under her tunic to grasp her hips and pull her core into the hard heat of his.

But Charlotte put her hands on his chest and pushed. 'No.'

'No?'

'No more running,' she said. 'You let me whisper all my secrets in your ear in the cave. It's time to whisper in *my* ear, Akeem.'

His nostrils flared, but he nodded, knowing that next time she wouldn't accept his attempts to divert her.

'I do not whisper, *qalbi*,' he said, and stalked back to the entrance of her room and opened the door wide. 'I roar.'

Charlotte remained silent. Breathless as she followed him up a staircase and down a long corridor.

Akeem came to a halt. 'Here it is.'

She frowned. 'A door?'

'A room.'

Her heart cinched. 'Your room?'

He shook his head.

She inhaled deeply, feeling regret or relief washing over her. She didn't know which. 'But I already have a room. Several.'

He reached for the handle. 'And now you have this.'

He pushed the door open and stepped aside.

Charlotte didn't move to touch him. She didn't dare. Because touching him would spiral her into a thousand splinters of emotions that would stream from her eyes in an unstoppable stream of— She inhaled deeply, trying to quiet her mind, to think. Of *delight*?

She whirled to face him. 'Why would you do this?'

'We will make this marriage work despite the circumstances that have brought us here, *qalbi*.' His eyes darkened. 'Your lessons begin tomorrow.'

Breathless excitement quickened her breathing. 'Lessons?'

'Your diploma,' he answered.

'But how...? Who...?'

'An artist in her own right, with substantial success in the European art world, and a retired teacher, is currently settling into her rooms. This—'

He waved his hands and her eyes moved across walls lined with different casings. A wide cupboard with thin slots holding different paper. Another with paints in bottles and tubes. Another with pencils, charcoal, and an array of other mediums.

'This will be your classroom.'

Her very own studio.

Hers.

'Why?'

'Proof,' he said. 'Your dreams will not be forgotten here.'

'What about your dreams?'

His eyes trained on her; Akeem stepped inside the room and closed it behind him with a flick of his wrist 'I dream to be the King my father wasn't.'

'Why? Why is it so important to be him? His heir, but not your mother's son? Why are you not both?'

He swallowed, pushing down the angst that had travelled with him throughout his life.

'The boy you speak of knew only one type of life. The care system embedded uncertainty into the little boy with scraped knees, too troubled to keep. Into the teenager too angry to place in a family home. He grew into a loner in the children's home. He was too quiet—too withdrawn—to engage in meaningful conversation. Too angry to soothe. The boy was unwanted. The teenager hated. The man…' He shrugged. 'He became a king.'

'I wanted the boy.'

'You wanted escape, *qalbi*. Not me. You wanted a new life away from your father. We are both grown enough now to recognise the truth.'

'You can't presume to know that.'

'I presume nothing. It is a truth I recognise. A truth that, if you wanted to, you would also recognise.'

'Tell me more about the boy who became a king,' she asked, moving on.

Or moving back.

He'd said enough in the cave. He did not want to go back.

'Tell me,' she urged, her voice soft. Tempting.

And there it was. The flare of kindness in her eyes, softening the green to a moss-like effect. Kindness. The reason he'd become besotted with her in their shared time in care.

His hands sought her out before he could tell them not to. They went to her hips, feeling the hard bones there as he tugged her into the length of him.

'All my life I wanted this "more" you talk of. And now I have it. I have it here—*power*,' he breathed between clenched teeth. 'The past is ir-relevant.'

'You want power?' she asked, and leaned into the pressure of his palms. 'Control?'

'I have it already,' he said, and loosened his grip. Because that was not the power he wanted. He did not want power over her.

She already has it over you.

He dismissed the voice and hammered his king-liness home. 'Power I imagined impossible is now mine. I have respect. Control.' He moved back, away from her. 'My mother's name was as un-wanted as mine before I was King. They called her a whore. And me a bastard. Only when I'd worked hard to be the perfect image of a crown prince did they call her by her name, and me by mine.'

'Your new name?'

He didn't answer.

'Whatever title you have, you'll always be him. You know that, don't you? Not the illegitimate legacy of your dad, or the result of whatever relationship your mum had with your father—'

'Don't.'

'I just don't understand how you think hiding away from who you once were makes you a better king.'

'Charlotte…'

'No!' She dismissed his warning. 'Your past isn't the enemy. Your dad lied to you. Like mine lied to me. Your feelings are valid. They make you strong.'

'Enough.'

'You said your dad was a terrible king. That he did not cater to the troubles of your people and followed his pleasure-seeking lifestyle and destroyed others in the process. You know the troubles of *real* people. Powerless people. First-hand. Why not tell them—*show them*—that because of your past you will be the King they need, if not the King they think they want.'

'They do not know what they want.'

'Then tell them—because they need you. Not this shell of a king, fighting against anything that might bring him joy—fighting against me.'

She lies. Feelings are not strength. Your past makes you vulnerable.

'My mother's name will always be in the gutter if I do not prove I am neither my father's son nor hers, but something else. Something stronger. *Better.*'

'You are strong,' she corrected him. 'You always were.'

He swallowed and closed his eyes.

'You can roar now, Akeem.'

He opened his eyes, his breathing coming faster and faster. 'Yes, I'll roar.' He jerked her forward with a snap of his wrists. Moved his hand up to caress the sensitive flesh at the base of her throat, swiping his thumbs against the erratic drum of her heart. 'And so will you.'

He pulled her with him, through one of the doors in the studio and then another adjoining door. He kicked it shut behind him. Everything in the room was a shadowed blur. All he could see was the bed. A huge, imposing four-poster of extraordinary wooden proportions.

Silently they walked towards the bed and he wasn't sure who was leading who. Only that they were here.

His bed.

A moan escaped her as he laid her down in the middle of the bed. Her hands moved on him, seeking an edge. She found it—the hem of his tunic—and lifted it up.

'I want to see you,' she said.

'I'm right in front of you.'

'I know…'

Her eyes held his, her hands against the flat of his stomach.

'I want to feel you against me. The man beneath those barriers of an adopted legacy.' She lifted the hem higher, exposing his hard, peaked nipples. She touched one. 'I want to see *you*.'

Groaning, he tugged off his tunic, throwing it to the floor. 'Touch me,' he commanded, and she did.

She touched him, placing her hot palm against his chest and stroking her fingers over him.

'You're perfect,' she said, running her fingers through the fine fuzz of hair to follow the ripples of his washboard chest.

She ventured lower. Tentatively moving her hands to his firm, full backside. Her hands stroked around the tense globes. She hooked her fingers into the band of his trousers and pulled, testing the elasticity.

His hands clasped hers and dragged them back up over his flat abdomen, raised them above her head.

'I've dreamt of this moment,' he confessed, leaving her hands to raise himself above her.

'Akeem!'

Eyes wide, Charlotte squealed as he gripped the seams of her tunic and tore it in two, ripping the fabric apart to expose her black lace-covered breasts.

He tugged the ripped top from her body and

bent to expose her golden flesh. He trailed his fingers down her upper arms. 'I've dreamt of being a king between your thighs,' he confessed. 'Extreme pleasure, surrounded by opulence.'

'And now?' she whispered.

Akeem set to work on her exposed throat. He kissed the arched tension from her neck slowly, tasting the sweetness of woman and the earthy, fresh sweat of passion. The slight tingle of salt on his tongue tempted him to suck deeper and bring her skin between his lips in a kiss that would mark her.

His mark.

She's already marked. And so are you.

Forcing himself to go slow, to stem the urgency demanding that he find her slick core and push inside her, he unhooked her bra.

'So beautiful,' he murmured, exposing her breasts and moving his mouth, licking and kissing the length of her collarbone, moving down to a dark nipple. He sealed his mouth over the puckered tip. Her moans grew faster, her nails digging in anywhere they could as he sucked her nipple deeply into her mouth while teasing the other beneath the pad of his thumb.

He flicked his tongue again and she quivered against him, panting hard. 'You are so responsive, *qalbi.*' He kissed and licked his way through the valley of her breasts.

'I want you....'

He raised his head. 'Say it again,' he commanded throatily.

'I want you, Akeem Ali, son of Yamina Ali.' Her eyes, green fire, thrust into him, inside him. 'And I want you too, Crown Prince, future King of Taliedaa.'

He lunged. She would have all of him. Take him deep. Until she didn't care who was inside her. The boy or the King. Only knew it was *him*.

He buried his mouth against her skin and kissed her harder, silencing the voice inside him and moving his mouth down her stomach. He kissed the waistband spanning her hips and tucked his fingers inside, then pulled the trousers off in one swift movement and threw them to the floor.

He returned to her. Positioning himself between her thighs, as the length of him found her core, he pressed against the entrance.

'Say yes,' he demanded, tilting his hips to apply more pressure.

One more nudge and he'd be inside her, and he needed her to tell him to push, to cement this moment with his body inside hers.

'Tell me this is what you want.'

'I need you, Akeem.' She wrapped her legs around his hips. 'Both of you.' The heels of her feet pressed into the dip of his lower back. 'Inside me.'

He swelled—his chest, his shoulders, his every

muscle expanding to accommodate the realisation that she was giving herself to him. *Completely.*

The room whirled around him, disappearing.

He thrust deep inside her.

'Akeem… Oh, Akeem!' Charlotte lifted herself and tilted her hips.

'Charlotte!' he cried as she brought him deeper inside her.

Her hands grabbed at him, pinching his flesh between her fingers as wave after wave of pressure ignited inside him, taking him to the edge.

She gripped his chin, making him look at her, and kissed him. It felt like a promise. A wordless pact. The way it had nine years ago. The night they'd shared then had been a promise.

He sank deeper inside her and he was lost. They both were. The boy and the would-be King were lost to Charlotte Hegarty.

And from the song of duty there was not a peep. Not a sound.

'Akeem!'

Charlotte sobbed into his shoulder, holding on to him as he pumped into her body, keeping his promise to bring her extreme pleasure.

But she couldn't see the opulence surrounding them.

She could only feel him.

The man she'd always wanted.

The man she'd never stopped wanting.

It was all-consuming and overwhelming. Because in nothing but their skin they were everything they had once been and everything they had become. They were nothing but a man and woman, seeking sanctuary in one another.

Escape.

He was her oasis and she was his.

That had always been the case.

But it's only sex, the broken voice in her head admonished. *Sex fixes nothing.*

The voice was right. Sex fixed nothing. Not even amazing sex. And this *was* amazing.

But love...love could.

She loved him.

She gasped at the realisation. Her limbs tightened, her legs curled around his hips, and her core clenched around his mass. Clenching and unclenching, she screamed, noisily urging him to love her faster—harder, because she loved the love of his body. And she loved him.

She made sense with him.

She always had.

Under the oak tree. In front of the TV. In rundown pubs. In helicopters across the desert. In nothing but her underwear on a throne. In a red ball gown. Against the cave wall. In his bed...

She loved the boy he had once been and the uncertain Prince he'd become under the veil of perfection—the persona of the perfect King.

Sex fixed nothing.

But love could.

And this was love, wasn't it?

And it wasn't neat or tidy.

'I'm— I'm—' She stuttered, because he'd exposed every nerve and she was burning with him in this ascent to the unknown as they travelled deeper into the oasis of their bodies, into their sanctuary—into each other.

He kissed her breasts, her neck, her mouth. 'Come for me, *qalbi*. Come now.'

And she did. A sheer blinding light burst behind her tightly closed lids and she let it claim her. The light. The brilliance. The release of love...of knowing she loved him. The shuddering climax was one only he could give her. Sanctuary in his body, and in his touch. The ultimate escape.

He roared, his neck straining backwards as he thrust one last time, filling her with himself. And she roared too. Loud and free.

He collapsed onto his elbows and she held him to her, his heart echoing the rapid pulse of hers.

For a long, breathless moment they stayed locked in each other's embrace, until their raging hearts slowed. Then he eased out of her and pulled her hips into his from behind, held her to him. He pulled the sheet over them.

'Sleep, *qalbi*.'

Safe in his arms—protected by the security of her love—she did.

CHAPTER TEN

THE BOY WAS still alive.

In him.

The illegitimate child of Yamina Ali was still breathing. Charlotte had pressed her lips to the lifeless body of a boy who belonged in the history books. She'd pressed her hand to his heart and pumped. Again and again. Until she'd seen a glimmer of life. And in his bed he'd been born again.

And now the boy was beating his fists against his chest. Demanding he recognise the fact that the woman who would walk through those doors towards him was more than a woman prepared to meet her King.

She was his.

He swallowed and fixed his gaze on nothing in particular. Not on the walls billowing with white drapes, drawn back to showcase the carved and intricate high arched windows, and not on the treacherous thump of his heart as the scent of foliage and flowers from every corner teased his nostrils.

He'd indulged her little game of playing in the past when he'd gifted her the studio. That night he'd let her draw him, with and without his clothes. He'd let her touch him without restraint, as he'd touched her. She'd whispered in his ear again and again about who they'd been, about family. She'd slept deeply. Contentedly. And for the first time in a long time so had Akeem—because he'd been home. The only home he'd ever really known.

Her.

The studio, making love and giving in to passion, confessing how his past had shaped him— *still shaped him*—had all been too much. It had made him weak. Put him in a position he'd vowed never to put himself in again.

So he'd returned her to her own bed. Because there were always choices. And he had made his. He'd left her alone after that afternoon which had turned into night and then to dawn. He'd buried his head in the duties of the King, and caged whatever man it was she'd released that afternoon.

Until today.

His wedding day.

The boy inside him howled like the feral beast he was—calling for her. Her presence. Her touch. Her soothing calm. But the boy could beat against his ribcage as much as he liked, because it was not his time.

It was time for the King to claim his bride.

He turned, ignoring the fact that his body—the howl inside his chest—knew she was behind him before his eyes did.

And there she was.

In her wedding dress.

His bride.

His Charlotte.

Gold feathered the cream veil covering her hair and shadowing her eyes. It ran over her shoulders and met in a high collar at her throat, tied at the neck by a string of gold between the notch of her clavicles. It trailed down her back in a short train. He could not see her face. Only the tip of her button nose and the shine of her full lips.

Her throat was bare, but panels of cream fabric embellished with sequins sewn in lines and swirls of silver hid every other inch of flesh. The embroidery at her midriff was a triangle, directing his gaze downwards. It ran the length of her torso and pulled in at her waist to mould over her hips, where more fabric flared out.

The dress sat against her body like a second skin, and every time she took a step towards him it moved tightly against the sway of her shoulders, flattened across the breadth of her thighs.

His eyes moved over the obvious lines of her thighs, her hip bones. He had gripped those— thrust inside her again and again until he'd forgotten his name. But he remembered it now: Crown Prince Akeem Abd al-Uzza, son of the late King Saleem Abd al-Uzza and soon to be King of Taliedaa.

Her promise pulled at his groin, but there was no escaping the cameras live-streaming their nuptials, or the princes, princesses and other dignitaries who surrounded them, who had travelled from the four corners of the earth to see the Crown Prince of an up-and-coming small desert kingdom take a bride.

After the ceremony there would be introductions, politics, food…

But after that…

One more night, the boy inside him urged. *Our wedding night.*

Yes. This would be his night. The night he'd promised himself in London. He would sleep with her one more time as a king with his queen. Seal their new pact. And then finally he would be rid of him. The boy she'd brought back to the surface—the boy who, after today, he couldn't risk remembering. He would put him back in his box and bury him deep. And then he would become the man he was destined to be.

The King that Taliedaa deserved.

What about her?

He'd give her the space to grow into the woman she was destined to be, too—a queen by day and an artist by night.

But his bed? He could not have her in it. He

could not let himself feel the way he did when she was there.

He dragged his eyes away from her—tore himself free from the lust threatening to undo him. The world and its eyes were on him—on *them*. He would do his people and his country proud.

And your mother?

An image of his mother's dark hair falling forward, obscuring her eyes, flashed in his mind. He could remember her scent. Her warmth. *Her love.* But he could not see her face. With every day that had passed since her death, she'd faded a little more.

Guilt. It passed through him in waves. As it always did.

He could not remember her now.

He moved his eyes over the crowds assembled in neat rows on either side of the aisle as Charlotte descended. Their eyes were not on their King, because they could not yank their eyes away from the display he'd gifted to them.

Her.

Their future Queen.

She stood before him and his heart jack-knifed as she pushed back her veil to reveal her eyes.

Her voice broke the bubble in the most delicate of whispers. 'I've missed you,' she said.

His mouth flattened as he took her elbow and turned them both to the man who would bind them together.

Eyes forward, he said, 'I've missed you too.'

God, help him. He had. So much.

She was born again as Crown Princess Charlotte Abd al-Uzza. Future Queen of Taliedaa.

She was married.

Excitement feathered over her skin, raising every fine hair under her wedding dress.

Tonight was the night.

He would be hers again, as he had been in the studio. In his bed. The man beneath the crown. Her Akeem. The Akeem he kept hidden from everybody but her. The man no one had noticed reaching for her when no one was looking.

He squeezed her hand as they chatted with some bigwig. He'd been by her side with every step, every introduction—every forkful of the delightful meal served at a table as long as her row of houses back home, covered in the crispest white tablecloth, the shiniest of tableware, seating an A-list of guests. He'd shown her with small gestures that, whatever disguise he was wearing, beneath he was the man in the studio. The man in his bed.

The man she loved.

A bell chimed and unseen hands flung the doors along the furthest wall open, bowing their heads.

The grand finale. Fireworks.

The crowds inside, who had already moved

from the banqueting hall into another room of equal lavishness, now moved outside.

Akeem's hand, with a firm hold on her elbow, guided her across the highly polished floor and out through the exit, down into the courtyard to the views of Taliedaa and the rolling hills of the desert under a night sky.

But he didn't stop. He walked past the crowds and past the views of his kingdom, through an arch in a high red stone wall, and unlocked a gate. He pulled her through, into another courtyard, and locked the gate behind them.

High walls surrounded them on either side. But at the heart of the courtyard was a low pool, scattered with underwater lights resembling candles. At its sides, pink-tinged columns of differing heights lined the cream-and-red-tiles. Everything glowed in warm tones of red and pink.

She craned her neck and saw that above them was a clear night sky. A single light flew into the sky with a whistle, and exploded above them in sprays of gold.

'Charlotte...' He moved in front of her.

The air shifted and she shivered. 'Akeem?' She took a step forward. 'You're here—it's *you*.'

'Here and in the flesh, Charlotte,' he confirmed.

Her eyes locked on to his lips, to those full brown lips making each syllable of her name sound...*right*.

And it *was* right—her name belonged in his

mouth. Because she belonged to him. She always had. To this man—the man beneath the crown. The man who had disappeared until their wedding day.

Her husband.

They appeared to be opposites, pulled together by an unseen power to stand face to face in the same disguise… But underneath…? Underneath, they were the same. They were each other's secret haven from the world outside. They always had been.

He dipped his head at the same time as she leant up. Their mouths met. The kiss was not perfunctory. Not the seal of commitment he'd offered to her in front of their guests. It was the kiss of a man kissing a woman. The same kiss that had met her in the studio—in his bed—when he'd surrendered to the past. To the intensity between them. *To her.*

And now he was surrendering again.

Hands grabbed and pulled at cloaks and veils until they lay discarded at their feet. They were primitive. Primal. They were *them* again. Everything they'd been that night in his bed.

She wanted him to roar again.

Now.

She cupped his face and kissed him deeper. Pushing her tongue into his mouth. Tasting him. Savouring him.

A trickling heat of a desire neither of them could deny burst between them.

Hard and unrelenting, his tongue probed, tasting her, skilfully dipping in and out the way his fingers had moved inside her in the cave. Releasing her wrists, Akeem slowed his kisses and moved to her neck. It was a slow assault of her senses as his hands moved over the sharp points of her hipbones and then flipped her around to face the wall.

'I can't wait,' he murmured, his voice tight and husked. He pressed a kiss to the underside of her ear. 'I need—'

'I need you too.' She placed her hands on top of his and guided them up her body to cover her breasts. 'I don't want to wait.'

He squeezed her breasts, pushing his hips into hers. The hard heat of him pressed into her and she moaned deeply as his mouth sucked at the sensitive part of her neck.

'Akeem…'

His hands moved from her breasts, down her ribcage and lower. He smoothed his fingers over her stomach, pressing into the pressure building there.

'Say it for me.' His fingers moved over the seams of her core, through her dress. 'Say please.'

'Please, Akeem,' she said.

Because it was his word, his face she saw when she said it, even with her face pressed against the wall. She pulled her hand away from his and reached behind her, finding the hard ridges of his thigh and then moving over to the hard heat of him. Stroking him. Up and down.

'Please,' she said again.

She stroked him faster, feeling him pulse beneath the black fabric of his trousers.

'Please...' She found his zip and caught the end of it, dragged it down. She eased her hand inside the opening and gently pulled him free.

'Lottie...' he moaned, and it fed her confidence. Fed her hunger to feel him hard inside her.

She smoothed her hand over the wet tip and closed her palm around his thickness. Smooth and hard. She pumped him.

'Please, Akeem, make love to your wife,' she said, and the words *your wife* made her heart race harder in her chest. They were a family now. By law. 'Make love to me,' she urged.

And he gripped the wrist of her hand that was working him, and the other one that lay on top of his hand working her, and dragged them both up her body, above her head, positioning them palm down on the wall on either side of her head.

'Wife...' he drawled against her cheek, and his hips pushed into her from behind, making her stomach press into the wall.

He flipped her hair over her shoulder and planted kisses to her nape as his hands trailed down her wrists to her elbows and back to her body, her waist. He grabbed her hips as his mouth moved with hard kisses down her spine.

On his knees, he reached for the hem of her dress and folded it upwards as he stood again, exposing her bare calves, her knees, her thighs. He rolled it all the way up until the dress sat on her hips, exposing her white lace-covered bottom.

His hands stopped, and she didn't move as she felt his eyes burning over her. This was her offering to him. Her surrender to the intensity between them.

'Wife...' he murmured again, and then he was on her. His hands moved between the apex of her thighs as she turned her mouth up to him and he claimed it. Kissing her hard as his fingers moved aside her panties until he found the pulsing heart of her.

'Mine!' he roared into her mouth. 'Wife!'

With his hand on her pulsing nub, he spread her legs open with his knee, grabbed her hips, and thrust into her.

'Akeem!'

'Husband,' he corrected.

He pumped into her and she couldn't catch her breath. She moaned too loudly, too fiercely. She was his. All his.

'Husband!' she roared, and she tightened her core, clenching around him. He was so deep. So completely a part of her...

They were here—despite everything and because of it.

They were married.

But did he want her? His wife? Could he love her? Not only her body, but *her*?

Could the King love his Queen?

Could she love them both, the man and the King? Love him enough to keep them together— their new family—if he didn't? If he couldn't love her back?

Her love hadn't been enough for her dad. Not enough to keep *that* family together. But this was her new family. *Theirs.*

She shut down the voice in her head. Let herself fall into the panting of their breath, the sealing of their mouths and bodies.

She broke free of his lips. 'Love me harder!' she begged. *'Love me!'* she cried. Because that was all she wanted.

His love.

He did not deny her. He loved her. *Hard.* And she met every thrust of his hips, backed herself into every entry of his hardness into her heat.

She shattered, falling against the wall, as wave after wave pulsed over her.

'Charlotte!' he roared. 'Wife…' he said. And with one last thrust he filled her with himself. Hot streams of love. And she came again. Shuddering against him as he leaned into her. She screamed loud as her orgasm, harder than the last, made her legs shake and her knees give way beneath her.

Breathless, he held her against the powerful wall of his chest, holding her up so she didn't fall. Just as he'd held her up in London, when she would have fallen into a wall of grief and despair. Just as he'd held her up on the plane. And now he was holding her up as his wife.

A firework of rainbow colours burst above them. Simultaneously, they craned their necks to watch the grand finale of their wedding day. An explosion of colour littering the night sky.

She couldn't help herself. She spoke.

'I love you.'

What had he done?

He eased out of her, steadying her on her feet, and with quick precision pulled her knickers back into place and rolled her dress down her thighs.

'Love?' he repeated and tugged up his fly.

For four days he'd resisted her. Resisted the need to bury himself inside her after that day in the studio—in his bed.

He was everything his father had accused him of being. A simple man with basic needs—and basic emotions. A man never in control, who lashed out with his tongue and didn't think of the consequences.

Your father showed you the consequences, didn't he?

'Love,' she agreed, turning to face him. Her beautiful face was flushed. Her lips swollen. 'You asked why I was helping you and I told you a half-truth.'

He wanted to ask about the other half, but he could not speak. His throat was too tight. His jaw was locked and his tongue was a dead weight in his mouth. She made him everything he didn't want to be—a man who followed his needs before his head. A man who consummated his marriage against a wall.

And she loved him? This weakness in him?

She was lying.

'The other half of the truth is love,' she continued. 'Not debts of gratitude or kindness. *Love*,' she emphasised. 'That will never change. I will always love you, Akeem. And I think a part of you will always love me. Because this marriage—'

'Is in the name of duty,' he reminded her.

'Is it?' she questioned gently. 'I think you already had everything in your possession to establish yourself as King.'

You didn't have her.

He clamped his lips together as she continued. 'The crowds cheered for you—not me. This marriage…you asked for it—demanded it—because somewhere inside you, you recognise the girl in me—inside this woman—who sees the boy in you.'

Her words made his skin itch. He wanted to claw at it. And at her version of what had happened. He wanted to rip it off his skin, pull it out of his ears, because it sat too neatly. Wrapped around him like something old and worn-in.

Something he already knew.

But he did not love her. He couldn't.

His black gaze intense beneath arched brows, he said, 'That boy does not deserve love.' And he didn't. He hadn't deserved it back when they were teenagers. And he did not deserve it now.

'Why not?'

She shivered, and his every instinct told him to pull her against him, pull her into his arms and crush her to him. Warm her up. He didn't.

'Everybody deserves love,' she said.

'No, not him. Not Akeem Ali. And not the King. They will never be allies. They are too different. Too—'

'Similar?' she interrupted. 'Because underneath all the noise they both want the same thing.'

'What do they want?'

'What we all want. To belong. To be a family.'

He reached down and collected her veil, held it out to her. 'You will freeze,' he told her, when she hesitated to accept it.

'I'd rather freeze than never hear your truth.'

'There is no truth, *qalbi*. There are only facts.'

'Then tell me the facts.'

'Love is never enough on its own—as my mother found out to her cost. Because love did not put food on the table. Love did not buy shoes for growing feet. Love did not pay for the car's MOT. Her love did not save her. My love couldn't save her.'

'She died in a car crash, Akeem. It was an accident. It had nothing to do with love.'

'I killed my mother,' he said, his voice level. 'The boy you are so determined to breathe life into killed her.'

'You were five—'

'I am the reason she is dead. That's how he made me remember. My father...' he breathed. 'Every time I questioned his choices he reminded me of mine. The basic nature of my conception. He said no family wanted me. Not even my own. Because I was primitive. I ate when I was hungry, cried when I was sad, shouted when I was angry. I had no control over my impulses because I was a boy with basic instincts—'

'Your father called you an *animal*?'

'Exactly. No better than a feral household pet that should have been euthanised at conception. Because my breed was primitive. And he was right.'

'He was wrong, Akeem. So very wrong.'

'Was he?' he asked. 'My mother worked until her knuckles bled—until she was so tired from feeding a boy who ate and ate. She died behind the wheel because she shouldn't have been driving.'

'He hurt you, didn't he? Your dad? I can feel it...' She placed her hand on her chest. 'In here.'

'My father wanted his heir on the throne, but he did not want his son. He did not want angry

Akeem. He beat his flesh to drive out everything he was.'

Appalled, she gasped. 'He hurt you *physically*?'

'No, not him. Not the King. But his men…'

Shame threatened to silence him, but he'd already said too much. And he was not ashamed that men twice the size of him with his eighteen-year-old body had hurt him. There had been too many to fend off.

It didn't matter. He was bigger now. Stronger. They wouldn't hurt him again.

He looked at her, at her too-big kind eyes. Pitying him. She couldn't hurt him again, either.

No, you're hurting yourself.

It wouldn't hurt. He wouldn't let it.

'I showed my father exactly who I was when I arrived. *Angry.* I demanded to know why he'd let my mother die… In answer, he had my clothes stripped from my body the minute I raised my voice. Bigger men, stronger men, held me and beat the angry teenager from me in front of him.'

And he'd controlled his anger every day since… controlled his impulses. Until her. Until he'd forgotten himself.

Her hand flew to her mouth, her eyes brimming with unwanted tears. But he would not touch her. He swallowed down his instinct to soothe her.

'I'm grateful my father had me beaten,' he continued, 'because he turned me into this. A prince.

He taught me control. To bury my impulses. To smother my feelings and—'

Are you a Daddy's boy now?

He was no one's boy.

Mummy's boy...

They'd called him that with every thump against his body the day he'd dared to question the King—dared to show him the angry teenager he was.

Mummy's boy.

'Your father taught you lies. Because all he taught you was to hate yourself,' she said, her voice heavy. Broken. 'Why didn't you leave?'

'Why didn't *you*?'

'Duty,' she answered. 'Duty to my dad.' She shook her head. 'Akeem…' she sobbed. 'Your dad was a villain too. But you didn't hurt your mum by living. You didn't kill her—that's ridiculous.'

'Yes,' he corrected. 'I did. If she hadn't chosen me—if she hadn't left Taliedaa—she would still be alive. She died so Akeem Ali could live. If I had left I would have been running away from my duty. I would have dishonoured my mother. Her people. They deserved more than my father was giving them.'

'*You* deserved more, Akeem,' she corrected. 'Your father…' She gasped—a sound he would not let deter him. She'd wanted this. But now she was stepping forward, arms outstretched.

'Do not touch me,' he said, because he could

not have her hands on him. Her softness against his rough. Her kindness…

Her mouth grappled soundlessly with unspoken words. Then she closed her eyes, inhaled a deep breath.

Softly, she spoke. 'He lied to you. He was selfish. He wanted what he wanted and made no allowances for anything else—any*one* else. He wanted an heir. He didn't deserve one. He didn't deserve *you*, Akeem Ali.'

'It is not that man—not Akeem Ali. I am the King my father taught me to be. With the new name he gave me. A new identity. I will carry my mother's memory on the shoulders of a king—not a beast who ruts in the dark and follows a basic urge to survive. Not this primitive man you make me.'

'There is nothing primitive or basic about you,' she denied with venom, pursing her lips and wrinkling her brow. 'You're more than instinct, Akeem. But instinct got you here. Got you through the life that was handed to you. If you were only built to react, you never would have survived the children's homes, the foster families, the social workers who talked about you in the third person. You should have broken, but you didn't even bend.'

He had broken. Had bent to his father's will. In order to forget everything that mattered.

The past matters, does it?

'My mother should have died at home, in her own country, in the desert where her heart belonged. And I am the reason she didn't.'

'Well, if that's true…' She blew out a heavy breath. 'Then we both killed our parents.'

'Nonsense. Your father killed himself.'

'We could go all the way back to my conception—'

'Stop it.'

'Or to my birth that drove my mother to drink more—'

'Stop.'

'Or we could go back to a few weeks ago, when I took an extra shift, didn't come home… I left him all alone and he died.'

'His death was not your responsibility—'

'And neither was your mother's yours. It wasn't your responsibility to protect your mother from herself. From her choices. You were a child. You are their child. But you are also your own man, and you're afraid to embrace that.'

'I fear nothing,' he lied—because he feared this. *Her love.* Her ability to look beneath his armour and make him question his mode of survival. 'I know the facts. The story does not matter. My story does not matter here.'

'Of course your story matters. It matters to me. So tell me and I will listen—like you listened to mine. Accepted mine. You are the son of a king, but you're also a man. A kind man. Just as you were a kind boy.'

'He was weak—'

'No,' she said firmly. 'That boy was kind.' She pointed at his chest. 'You are kind. You took me to your secret haven. You gifted me my dream. *My art.* Knowing I was all alone, you travelled to London to get me. You forgot your duty and dropped everything for me. You are everything that came before in *your* story. Not theirs—not your parents' story.'

She moved into his space and grabbed his hand. He let her take it.

'*That* is the man I love,' she said, 'and I don't care what his name is any more. Because you are him and I lo—'

'Do not say it again.'

She ignored him. 'I love you.'

She must be all out of bullets because they did not penetrate his skin. Her presence. Her words. He wouldn't allow them in. He would not be that man in the studio, roaring his secrets into her body. He would not be the man thrusting into his wife against the wall.

He could only be one man, and she wouldn't let him be him.

There was only one choice to be made.

He would let her go.

'You might care,' he said. 'And you might

choose a completely different name when I tell
you why I came to London.'

'For me,' she answered. 'For closure.'

'I came for you,' he agreed, 'but not for closure.'

'Then for what?'

'I came to crush you.'

Instinct told him to draw her nearer, but he
pushed her away. She could take her love with her.

'Crush me how?'

Her voice was small, but it needled him. The
strength in her eyes was telling him she could
take what he gave her. That she knew what he
was doing and wouldn't allow it. But he wouldn't
give her a choice. This hunger, this desperation
between them, was…weakness.

'Revenge.'

He let the word sit with her. Watched it penetrate. Felt the tremble of her fingers in his palm.

'My dad—'

'You pushed for this, Charlotte. Ever since you
arrived here you have pushed me to confront the
past—what it means to me, how it shaped me.
So you will take it. You will understand how the
past—our shared past—drove me dizzy with the
need to pluck you from your life and thrust everything I am in your face. To tease you—tempt
you—and then snatch it all back when what you
craved was me. Throw you back into your pitiful life. I wanted to crush you under the weight

of my power. The power of the Crown Prince. Of the King. Of *me*.'

'That's not who you are.'

'That is exactly who I am.'

He knew it now, and he knew what he must do to become the King his people needed. No temptations from the past. No whispers in the night about a person he could never be again. Because she was right. He was a man in his own right, and today he would embrace it.

Today he would let them all go.

'Are you sufficiently crushed, *qalbi*?'

'No.'

Her response was barely audible. Everything he had become over the last nine years stared at her. Not at the girl she was. Not at the Queen he had made her. But at the woman in a wedding dress. The woman determined to change him. To make him *feel*...

He felt nothing.

'You won't be free until you confront what hurts you,' she said. 'And I want to be here when you do. But if you can't...if you can't reach out and take what's in front of you...*me*—all of me.' She swallowed, the delicate tendons in her throat tightening. 'Then I'll walk away.'

He would not reach out.

He couldn't.

He couldn't be with her. Not when she questioned the very fabric of who he was—who he'd turned himself into. A king. She regarded his crown with disdain. His riches—his power—she treated them as if they were nothing. As if *he* was nothing—an empty shell surrounded by opulence. Everything he'd wanted to prove to her that he was...*meant nothing to her.*

She wanted the past—a boy long forgotten. She did not want him. She did not want the man he'd become. She wanted to stay in her basic world of having to *make do* even after everything he'd shown her—rubbed in her face.

He would never make do again.

He wouldn't be basic.

'Then walk—I won't stop you,' he said, and his voice was not his own. 'I cannot be this man you seek because I am not him. I will never be him again.'

She didn't say a word. She turned her back on him and opened the gate. With her veil obscuring her face and her dress clenched around her midriff. She walked away.

She was a liar.

She hadn't run with him. She'd run away. Like they all did. Because no one wanted angry Akeem. Hurt Akeem. Broken Akeem.

The rope snapped.

Untethered and alone, he sank to his knees.

Charlotte crashed into her room and leant against the door, drawing deep, long breaths into her tight lungs.

The truth was out. He didn't want their past. He didn't want her. Not the woman she was now. Not the woman he'd given her the choice to become. She couldn't stay here. She couldn't give herself to a man who only shared the physical side of himself.

She couldn't. She couldn't be part of a one-sided relationship ever again. Her relationship with her dad had taken everything from her and given nothing in return. He'd convinced her she had nothing to give to anyone else. Not even herself. She would not do it again. She would not open herself up to be shot down—to be shown she wasn't worthy of respect.

Of love.

Selma hurried towards her, her hands splayed, her eyes wide. 'Charlotte!' She came closer, gathering her against her. 'What has happened? Why are you here? You are trembling.'

She was trembling—but not because she was cold. Because he'd broken her. Her heart.

She'd pushed too hard—too quickly.

'Let's clean you up,' Selma said, and pulled her into step beside her.

She leant on her shoulder and walked to the bathroom with Selma holding her up. She was grateful for the support because she was ready to fall, to pull herself into a ball and weep. But that was the old Charlotte. This Charlotte would walk away with her head high. However much it hurt.

And it wasn't a pitiful existence that she'd return to. For all his cruel words, he had fixed her. Wrapped her in the light of hope. And she would cling to it. She would continue to chase her dreams. Her diploma. She would be all the things she wanted to be—with or without him.

She stopped walking and took Selma's hands in hers, grasped them tightly. 'I need your help,' she said, her stomach flipping upside down and inside out.

'Of course.' Selma squeezed her hands back, just as tightly. 'Anything.'

She'd never had a friend other than Akeem, but now she had Selma, and she could cry for the girl who had never known this.

Friendship.

She'd thank her later.

Charlotte steeled herself to ask for what she needed to do next and then asked it, pulling the words out of her throat and spreading them into the air.

And it hurt.

'I need you to help me leave the palace.'

CHAPTER ELEVEN

SHE WAS QUEEN—of course he knew where she was. Did she think he didn't? The moment she'd left the grounds a guard had spoken in his ear. They'd followed her—for her own safety, of course—told him she was safe with Selma.

He hadn't chased her because he'd been right to push her away. To let her go. He'd been right because the moment she'd seen it—*him*—she'd run. He'd been right to tell her he couldn't love her. Because how could he love her when he didn't love himself?

You're nothing without her.

'Leave me,' he said, in answer to the soft rap at the door. A rap that had come three times a day for six days. Today was the seventh. Today was the day he would officially succeed to the throne without his Queen.

'Highness…' The voice was hesitant, but still his senior aide ventured across the threshold.

'Leave me.'

'You must ready yourself—'

'I *am* ready,' he replied, without looking at or acknowledging the tray of refreshments that was being placed on the low table by the door even as another, untouched one, was removed.

He'd been readying himself for this for nine years. What did he have to prepare that he did not already know by heart? By rote? A few practised words, a bow, a crown, a new title.

King.

But wasn't he already King in every way that mattered? Did he not already rule them? Lead them? Had he not led them when his father had been busy, distracted by his latest obsession?

Hadn't he shown them he was worthy to be their King? Hadn't he, to become the King they needed, shown that the past had no place in this world? Hadn't he shown her there was no place for either of them? Because he, the forgotten orphan heir—soon to be the ruler up on high—couldn't be King with any ties to the past, to the emotional boy now in front of him, staring at him with big brown eyes.

His eyes.

His legs cramped beneath him and he shifted, splaying them out flat. He looked again. Stared at the easels lined up against the windows overlooking the city. *His* city. Pictures by Charlotte—of him. Her drawings of a life he'd tried to forget and a life he was barely living.

So many of them…

Him at the children's home, under the oak tree. Him asleep in a small single bed. Her at her bedroom window in London as he looked up at her from below. Both of them together, locked in an embrace surrounded by fire in the cave—his secret oasis. Both of them on the balcony… And a double portrait. A boy and a would-be king, side by side, staring straight back at him with the same brown eyes.

He'd swapped one life for another, hadn't he? Without claiming either? Neither of those lives— the boy's or the King's—belonged to him. He'd been a puppet of the system until his eighteenth birthday and then he'd been his father's puppet, claiming a heritage he'd never known belonged to him and changing himself to repair a legacy he hadn't broken. His father had. And yet *he* had claimed the responsibility.

But at what cost?

'The ceremony starts in two hours.'

'Please, leave.'

'As you wish.' Resigned, his aide complied.

The door closed silently behind him—Daniyal, his right-hand man, and he couldn't bring himself to care about his unkindness. Kindness had brought them all down. It had brought *her* down. His Charlotte. His Queen. His wife…

No, you brought her down.

He had.

He looked down at the aged paper in his hands.

He'd found the picture Charlotte had drawn of him in care. He'd found it in a suitcase battered from his time in the children's home.

The suitcase was scuffed from trailing it behind him to every temporary home he'd spent time in. He hadn't even unpacked it when he'd arrived in Taliedaa.

Because you expected to leave again, like every time before.

Exactly! He hadn't unpacked it in those foster homes, because he had known those big smiles and open arms were fake. Those hands hadn't been reaching for him. They'd been reaching for the cheque they'd be given at the end of his stay. A brief stay before they sent him back with the same suitcase.

His father had been reaching for a legacy. His name. His lineage. His continued bloodline. Not his son. So he hadn't unpacked again.

He clenched his fists too tightly. Then he prised his fingers open and felt his insides twist.

It was the first portrait she'd ever drawn of him, and she'd gifted it to him as a thank-you. *Thank you?* He'd destroyed them both with his weakness. He'd left her behind and now he'd thrown her back into her old world because he was an indecent bastard. His father had been cruel and selfish. Her father had been a mean drunk. But he was something worse. Maybe her father had been right—maybe he was a monster.

What have you done?

He laid the paper out flat on the floor, trying to smooth the creases his destructive hands had crunched into it. But he only blurred the lines. Smudged the face of the boy she'd drawn.

He destroyed everything.

Everything good.

Blew out the light of hope.

Hadn't he been to blame for never finding a home? He'd never given anyone a chance to want him. He'd never given Charlotte a chance to love him.

It was your fault nine years ago too, wasn't it?

The voice was right.

It had been his fault. The blame was solely at his feet.

Because he'd let her go. He'd believed the lies that seemed so brittle when he thought of them now. Her father's words. The trickery. But he hadn't been tricked. He'd allowed himself to believe those lies because he'd been afraid. Afraid of her. Her presence. Her stray bullets. Her kindness.

Her love.

He looked at her pictures again. She was everywhere in the studio. In the portraits lining the walls. On the sofa, where her shawl spread out haphazardly. In the lids left open. The drying paintbrush by the sink.

You're still afraid, aren't you? To show them who you are?

Instantly, he saw everything.

Everything she'd been trying to show him.

She'd drawn his story. The story he'd pushed down into that place where he'd hidden everything that mattered.

He'd forgotten to keep the parts that made him *him*.

He was both.

A boy in the body of a king.

That rope…it hurt. It always had. For nine years. But now… It had snapped. Irreparably. She'd gone because he'd pushed her away…because he'd refused her encouragement to be himself.

He loved her.

He'd sat here for a week. Sat here on the floor, in her studio, in sky-blue jeans ripped at the knees, and a T-shirt so thin and tight it defined every muscle beneath. Clumsy fingers had repaired the socks on his feet. *His* fingers. And the shoes he hadn't been able to bring himself to slide his feet into had lasted him three winters in the coldest temperatures the British weather could offer. They were almost soleless now.

He jumped to his feet.

He could not drag her back to the palace and demand she listen to him. *Forgive him.* He needed to show her. He needed to show them all. But would she come? Would she come to see him named King before his people?

He didn't know, but he needed to do it. Not just

for her, but for himself. His father had never listened to his people, never given them the privilege of choice. But he would let them choose now.

He would let them choose *him*.

But first he would change. He was no longer this boy with ripped jeans—he was both a boy with a challenging past and the son of a king. And they both deserved finery. Top-of-the-range quality fabric...

They were both worthy of *more*.

It never lessened. The lurch in his gut as he looked down over the city below... But it was one face he looked for amongst the crowds gathering outside. *Hers.* And she was everywhere and nowhere.

Striding towards the door, he pulled it open, ignoring the bowing men and the curtsying women. He moved through the winding halls laden with pictures of ancestors he would never meet and stepped out into the day.

In the flower-adorned courtyard with its sound of cascading fountains Akeem didn't stop. His face stony, he entered the royal gardens.

He shrugged off the staff, directing him back inside to the royal balcony. He wouldn't be there. He would not stand up there and look down at them.

He would stand amongst them. *His people.*

He would tell them a story. *His story.*

He would give them the choice his father never had.

'I came to you nine years ago with nothing…'

They'd taught him how to project his voice, to make it boom in the loudest arena. It boomed now. The people surrounding him moved away, creating a circle around him and giving him space.

'I was a stranger to your ways…' he continued, keeping his voice neutral.

He was not neutral. He was alive. Breathing. His royal guard infiltrated the crowd and discreetly made the space between him and his people wider. He continued and spoke to them too—to the royal guard, his inherited men—because they needed to hear his words too.

'I was a stranger to the personal struggles of this Kingdom of Taliedaa. But I am not a stranger to struggle or to hunger. Not only for food, but for the warmth of stability. I was a man when I came to you—when I stood above you in fine silks and asked you to accept me. And you did. Because my father asked you to—he demanded it. I thought on that day I had left the boy I was behind. But my wife…your Queen-in-waiting…has reminded me that that boy's struggles—his losses—are universal. I have lost much, and so have many of you.'

Pain sliced through him, but he would raise his mother's memory up—the memory of who she had been, not who he had turned her into. The woman—the mother—he had forgotten.

'My mother… She was a young mother. A single mother in a foreign land, who worked her fingers to the bone to raise me. Her son. In my early life she wrapped me in hope, in love, in warmth, and I did not hunger because of her. She was one of you. Born here, raised here. *Loved* here. Until she made a mistake and fell in love with a king. And I am that mistake. It shamed her. *I* shamed her. Forced her to leave all she'd known because of her love. Her warmth. Her desire to see her son flourish. Now I ask all of you—would you not do the same? For love? Would you not abandon everything you'd known to raise your child? She did. She did not allow me to live in shame. My mother, Yamina Ali, raised a king.'

Oh, how his heart thundered. Beat painfully against his ribs. No, it was not his heart. It was the boy. Charlotte had removed his gag.

'My wife, Charlotte Hegarty, left behind her life to make a home here—for her love of your Crown Prince.'

Oh, he felt it now. *Love.* All around him. In every caress…every word. She had not let him forget just because he had not taken the good parts with him. She had shown him he needed the good parts of his past.

He needed her most of all.

'The Queen understands struggle,' he continued. 'She also understands what it means to overcome it. She has kept her promise to you. She has offered comfort and support to your Crown Prince. She has reminded me why I can be the

King you need, if not the King you want, because your struggles are my struggles. And unlike my father, who stood above you in fine silks and then shut you out, closed the doors and forgot about you, I will not forget. Akeem Ali, the son of Yamina Ali and the late King Saleem Abd al-Uzza stands here today along with your Crown Prince. Because I am both in one body—in one flesh—and I will not choose one over the other.'

There it was, all out in the open, and he did not feel shame. He felt lighter. Better. Stronger than he ever had. But he needed to know. He needed his people to tell him… And even if the answer was not what he hoped for, at least he would have given them the choice. The choice of who was their King, their leader, regardless of blood or legitimacy. It was their right to choose and he would give them the choice his father hadn't when he'd thrust him upon them.

He would ask them now.

'Do you want me—this half-man, half-son-of-a-king—to be named your leader today? Your King? Because it is your choice and yours alone, people of Taliedaa. I will not demand to be King as my father did. So, tell me now, is this Prince of both worlds enough? Is he who you want to lead you into the future? Because I can be no one else? I am Akeem Ali Abd al-Uzza.'

The crowds roared.

He was their King.

He saw her then. Not her face, but her eyes. A simple black headscarf covered her hair and her face, and a black dress fell to her ankles.

But it was her.

She was here.

Running with him…

Charlotte slid back the scarf.

He moved, and the crowd parted, and then he stood before her. Before his wife. His Queen. He had no words left. None. So he dropped to his knees and swore his allegiance to her. To the only woman who had cared enough to see him.

The true him.

The man and the King.

Akeem Ali Abd al-Uzza.

For nine years she'd wanted him on his knees. And now he was, Charlotte did the only thing she could. She got down on her knees too.

'The new King,' she said, in her newly found authoritative voice, even though her insides were trembling. She bowed, her chin to her chest, her knees turned to stone. 'Akeem Ali Abd al-Uzza—rightful heir to the throne.'

His hand sought hers. His fingers pushed through hers. And she let them.

Together, they raised each other up.

The surrounding crowds roared.

She hadn't intended to stay in Taliedaa, but she hadn't been able to leave. Leaving the palace with

Selma, travelling into the city…every step had been agony. Every step taking her away from him. She hadn't been able to bear it—the thought that another decade might pass before she saw him again. *If* she saw him again. So she'd stayed close to Selma. Hidden in plain sight.

She hadn't intended him to see her today—hadn't wanted him to think she was there because of duty, to hold the hand of the Crown Prince. Because the King didn't need her to hold his hand. He would be the King with or without her. She was here for Akeem the man. To offer her support even if he didn't know it was there.

But she was holding his hand anyway—and he was holding hers.

His expensively tailored black suit was moulded to every inch of his body, a golden tie was at his throat, and he was every inch a king, surrounded by opulence, with the power of the people in his hand. But not because of his lineage, because of *him*.

The man they had never seen coming.

The only man she had ever loved. Still loved.

The boy and the man. Both in the same skin. Her husband the King.

She leant into him and whispered, 'I'm proud of you.' And she *was* proud of him. Proud of him for embracing who he was and what he could become.

Black eyes held hers, and she saw herself in their reflective depths.

Did he want her there—inside him? Because he'd always been inside her. He'd never left.

Wordlessly, he took her elbow and led her inside. And she let him walk her in with fear in her stomach.

This might be the last time he guided her anywhere.

This could be their last goodbye.

She would not cry.

The doors closed behind them and she inhaled a stunted breath.

'I'm sorry,' he said.

She closed her eyes. Her heart was pumping too loudly. *He was sorry?* She waited for the excuses, for him to turn his wrongs into hers... Because where there was pain, wasn't it always her fault? Hadn't life taught her that not everyone could own their mistakes without hurting others with their reluctant apologies?

She waited until she couldn't wait any more. She opened her eyes.

'Say it again.'

He didn't hesitate. He dropped to his knees. 'I'm sorry, Charlotte. I'm sorry I hurt you. I'm sorry I was too stupid to see that those moments in the cave, in the palace and in my bed—' he swallowed, jutting out his lower lip '—were the only moments where I revealed the true me to anyone. You saw me even when I didn't want you to.'

He knelt motionless, still but for the heavy rise and fall of his chest.

'I couldn't tell you my name because underneath it all—the opulence and the power I'd longed to rub in your face—I was no one. An empty vessel of nothing. A mass of broken flesh and bone. I'd swapped one life for another without claiming either for myself. Neither of those lives—the boy's or the King's—belonged to me. I was a puppet of the system until my eighteenth birthday, and then I was my father's puppet. Thank you, Charlotte,' he finished, and every line on his face was taut. Pained. 'Thank you for setting me free.'

She so badly wanted to jump into his arms, to tell him she was right here, with him, and she was going nowhere. But words were cheap. His words outside had been for himself, for his people. But now she wanted words for her. Proof that he could embrace the past—because it was the only way they could move on together.

So she didn't raise him up. And she didn't feel victorious, and neither did her sixteen-year-old self. She felt...*abandoned.*

He might not have abandoned her on purpose nine years ago, but he'd abandoned her on their wedding night.

Would he abandon her again?

'What will you do with your newfound freedom, Akeem?' she asked. 'What will you do with *me*?'

Her heart was beating so hard because he

didn't need her any more. Not to be his Queen.
His wife. But did he want her? Did he need her as
she needed him? As a lover? A friend? Family?

'I want to love you hard…'

His eyes flashed and her stomach pulled. That
night he'd loved her fiercely with his body but
abandoned her with his mind.

'So hard,' he continued, 'that you are breathless with my love.'

'I'm not talking about sex.'

'And neither am I.' He swallowed, searching her
face as she searched his. 'I thought my riches, my
power, would make you want me.' He held up his
huge hand, the slender digits halting her rebuke.
'I was wrong. You cared for none of it. Not even
for a diploma.' He smiled, oh, so weakly. So tentatively. 'In the cave you asked if I was worthy.'

'Are you?'

'The man before you is worthy. I am worthy of
love. I am worthy of the happiness I find in your
arms, in bed, against the wall or on the floor,
or simply by being in your presence while you
sleep…watching you draw.' He hushed her again
when she tried to speak. 'But more than that we
are worthy of happiness, Charlotte. Of love.'

'Love?' she repeated. She wanted—no, she
needed to touch him. But she didn't.

'Love,' he agreed. 'All week I have wanted to
drag you out of Selma's house in the city. Drag you
into my bed and love you so hard you wouldn't

be able to leave my bed for days. Because sex is what we do—how we talk.'

His Adam's apple moved up and down his taut throat.

'I wanted to keep you in bed for weeks,' he went on. 'For however long it took you to forgive me. Instead…' he said, and then he exhaled heavily, a shudder escaping his lips. 'Instead I sat in your studio. I sat there on the floor and stared at your drawings—your portraits. Of me. In the cave. On the balcony. In the children's home… And the double portrait.' He exhaled heavily. 'You were the only one to ever see me when I was standing in plain sight. I want to be the man you see. I can't make you forgive me, but I can promise I will talk with my mouth, as well as with my body. I will use my words and my actions to show you how much I love you. How sorry I am for not listening. For making you pack a box with your feelings.'

'I never really packed it,' she confessed wryly, and her heart was so light—so full—she could burst.

'I want to unpack mine, and then I want us to fill a fresh box—without a lid. I want us to fill it with the intensity between us. I've tried to deny that I feel it, but it has never diminished. It has only grown. Grown into an all-consuming need to be in your presence. To touch you. Be with you. Love you. And I don't want to deny it any more. I want to keep it in a place where we can both see it, feel it, embrace it. Use it to drive each other to be better. *Stronger.* Because it was never a weakness. You are my strength, Charlotte. You make me a better and stronger man.'

She rushed to him. Fell to the floor with him and landed in his arms. She scrambled with the too-long light cotton sleeve and unbuckled the watch. Her heart pumping. Her eyes too wide. She grabbed his wrist, pushed up his sleeve and attempted to wrap the delicate watch around his wrist. It was too tight. It looked ridiculous. She pushed the fine silver pin through the last hole.

Perfect.

'She's been here today with you...your mum.'

'I know,' he whispered.

'Your dad too, watching his people. And my dad—' She choked. 'He was here as well.' She grabbed his hand and placed it on her chest. 'In here.

'There were two sides to your father,' she told him, because she got it now. Understood it for what it was, right or wrong. 'There was the man who abandoned you, and there was the King. Your father the King moulded every sentence you spoke today.'

'How do you know that?'

'My dad had two sides as well. The side social services saw, so he could get me back home, and the side he showed to me. Maybe getting me back was in his eyes doing the right thing. Standing by his duty. The way your father stood by his in the end. He was cruel, but he came for you. Turned you into a king. I hate him for how he treated you, but he was still your dad.'

'Determined as ever to compare our lives, Charlotte?' said Akeem.

'We walked the same streets in the same shoes once, didn't we? I can see your path as clearly as I can see my own. Your father made you a king, and your mother made you emphatic and compassionate.'

'And your father made you strong. Invincible against all odds.'

'For all his faults, I am his daughter. And I loved him.'

'I cannot say I loved my father, but I loved my mother. I loved her so much—' His voice broke, and she finished for him.

'It was easier to blame yourself, to be angry, than to let yourself grieve.'

'Yes,' he said, his eyes heavy with unshed tears. 'I see that now.'

'Love is not the enemy. Life can be hard sometimes, and then at other times it can be...*magical*.' She smiled. 'As magical as fire when your eyes aren't accustomed to the dark.'

'I want to be your light in the darkness, *qalbi*. I want to be your oasis when all around you is sand.'

Together, they said, *'Sanctuary,'* and laughed. Her hands moved to the back of his neck and she toyed with the hair at his nape. 'Are you scared?' she asked.

'Yes,' he said.

'It's okay to be afraid when everything is changing.'

'Is it, *qalbi*?'

'Yes—because what you're feeling is growing pains.'

'Do you feel them too?' he asked.

'Yes,' she smiled weakly. 'And it hurts. But I want to hurt with you. Change with you. Grow with you. Love you.'

'I'm not afraid of my feelings any more,' he told her. 'I'm not afraid of this. Of us. Of what we are.'

'And what are we?'

'Husband and wife.'

'King and Queen?'

'We are both and we are more.' He tugged her into his arms. 'We are family.'

'Family,' she agreed, and let the tears fall.

'Qalbi...' Big, solid hands came about her waist and pulled her into him. 'My heart,' he said.

Akeem tilted her face to search her eyes. And he saw himself in them. The man and the King, on the floor in her arms.

'Call me by my name, my heart,' he demanded, with everything he had been, with everything he was, and with everything he would become. 'Tell me I am yours.'

'Akeem. The boy of my dreams, the man of my heart,' she whispered. 'Husband. King. Mine.'

He kissed her, and she kissed him.

It was a promise.

A promise of today, tomorrow and for ever.

* * * * *

Swept up in the magic of
His Desert Bride by Demand?
Watch out for Lela May Wight's next story.
Coming soon!